FORTUNE COOKIE

Jean Ure

HarperCollins *Children's Books*

For Emily Collins and

Katherine Story

First published in Great Britain by HarperCollins *Children's Books* in 2009
HarperCollins *Children's Books* is a division of HarperCollins*Publishers* Ltd,
77-85 Fulham Palace Road, Hammersmith, London W6 8JB

The HarperCollins *Children's Books* website address is
www.harpercollins.co.uk

7

Text © Jean Ure 2009
Illustrations © HarperCollins*Publishers* 2009

The author and illustrator assert the moral right to be
identified as the author and illustrator of this work.

ISBN-13: 978-0-00-722462-3

CHAPTER ONE

Hi! I'm Fudge Cassidy, and this is my friend, the Cupcake Kid. She's my bestie!

There's a photo of us that Cupcake's mum took last year, when we'd just started at secondary school. We're showing off in our new school uniforms, which we now wouldn't be seen *dead* in. Not if we could help it. We are both smiling proudly, looking straight at the camera. Nothing to hide! No guilty secrets. That all came later...

Cupcake's the thin one. The one with the long, dark hair tied in a plait. I'm the short, stubby one with all the freckles. Not to mention the blobby nose, which Dad always says looks like a button mushroom. Cupcake has a really nice nose! Sort of... *noble*. She complains about it being too long; she says it's like a door knocker, but I'd sooner have a door knocker than a mushroom. I think people show you more respect.

Another thing Cupcake complains about is her teeth. They are being trained not to stick out, which means she has to wear a brace, which sometimes makes her sort of *buzz* and *click* when she says certain words. Mostly ones beginning with S. I have never told her, but when she first had the brace and started buzzing and clicking I thought it was really cool and wished that I could have one! I did suggest to Mum that

FORTUNE COOKIE

maybe I ought to, "just in case". Mum said, "Just in case what?" I said, "In case my teeth start growing outwards. I think they *are* starting to... look!" And I pulled this bunny face with my bottom lip sucked in, just to show her. But Mum never takes me seriously. She says I'm too impressionable and always getting these crazy ideas.

"There's nothing the matter with your teeth! Don't be so daft."

I bet Cupcake's mum wouldn't tell her to put her teeth away and not be daft. Well, she obviously hadn't. *She'd* taken her to the dentist to get a brace put on, which is what any normal mum would do. Not mine! "No," she says, when I remind her of it, "I am a hard woman."

Cupcake's mum isn't hard; neither is Cupcake. They are both very caring sort of people. In fact, Cupcake is nothing but a great big softie, which is what I'm always telling her. If Cupcake takes after her mum, I s'ppose I ought to be honest and admit that I probably take after mine. I do love my mum (in spite of her not letting me have a brace) but I just HATE it when people look at me and go, "Ooooh, don't you look like your mum!" I mean, nobody wants to look like their mum, right? If they said, *Don't you look like*................... (fill in the name of your favourite celeb). Well! That'd be different. But I don't expect anyone's favourite celeb is likely to be short and stubby with a button mushroom instead of a nose, and a face covered all over in splodgy brown freckles. Yuck yuck yuck!

Now I've gone and lost track. I'm always doing that! Attention span of a flea. That is what Mrs Kendrick said to me last term, and I guess she might be right. My mind does hop about a bit! What I really meant to do was write about me and Cupcake. Say how we first met. How we got to be friends. That sort of thing.

OK! Me and Cupcake first met when our mums were in the hospital, right next to each other in the ward. How cool is *that*? Cupcake was born a whole half-hour ahead of me without any fuss at all, and afterwards she just lay there gurgling in her crib, as good as gold, so that everyone ooh-ed and aah-ed and said what a sweet little baby she was. I *apparently* was all loud and red and screaming and kept sicking up over everything and generally making a nuisance of myself. I don't suppose anyone ooh-ed and aah-ed over me. They probably took one look and jumped back in horror, going "Aaaaargh! Save me!"

Once, when I was trying to discover a bit more about those ancient times, I asked Mum if she could have told which baby was me and which baby was Cupcake if we hadn't had those little wristband things with our names on – cos, you know, all babies look alike when they are first born. Well, I think they do. I wouldn't be surprised if all kinds of mistakes are made. Mum seemed to find this amusing. She said, "We never had the *least* trouble telling you apart!" She said that Cupcake was always "such a dear little soul... so good and quiet and eager to please." Unlike me, is what she meant! I guess it's true, me and Cupcake are just, like, totally different — which doesn't stop us being in-sep-ar-able. Like, *joined at the hip*, as people say, though I'm not quite sure why. If we are joined anywhere, it's at the shoulder. We go round all the time with our arms round each other. Either that, or linked together. Sometimes it's like we're stuck with glue! It's strange to look back and remember that it hasn't always been like this.

After we'd got born, and our mums had taken us back home, we didn't see each other again for ages. Years and years. Nine, to be exact. I was in Year 5 when Cupcake suddenly turned up at my school. We didn't know we'd already met! After all, it wasn't like we'd been properly introduced or said hi, or anything. So to begin with, the first few days, we didn't really take much notice of each other. I thought Cupcake was a bit boring, to be honest. All mousey and miserable. She didn't ever seem to laugh, or join in any of our games at break time. Just skulked round by herself, looking like a tree had fallen on top of her, with her shoulders hunched and her head way down. No fun at all! She confessed later that she hadn't liked me any more than I had liked her. She said I was all loud and bossy. "A right show-off!"

Thing is, Cupcake had a reason to feel sad. I didn't have any reason for being loud and bossy. I think my voice just naturally comes out as a bit of a bellow; Mum is for ever telling me not to shout. As for being bossy — well, maybe I *sometimes* am. But not on purpose! I just get kind of carried away. Same with showing off. I never mean to. "No," says Cupcake, "you just *do*." But she has learnt how to squash me! And she has learnt how to laugh, in spite of everything. I like to think this is partly thanks to me.

It wasn't till she had been in school several days that our mums arrived at the same time one afternoon to collect us and surprise, surprise! They recognised each other. That was when we discovered that we had already met. Our mums immediately started swapping memories. Cupcake's mum remembered how I hadn't seemed to want to be born — "You were *so* overdue!"

– and my mum told us how Cupcake had been such a *quiet* little baby and how I had been the noisy one.

I remember me and Cupcake exchanging glances. I was thinking, "Quiet just means *boring*," while Cupcake was thinking, "She still is noisy." I know this is what she was thinking cos ages afterwards she actually told me.

It turned out that Cupcake and her mum were living just two minutes away from us. I was not exactly overjoyed when I first realised this, and I don't expect Cupcake was, either. I nearly shrieked when we got indoors and Mum said, "Isn't that lovely? Meeting up again after all this time! I do hope you'll become friends."

I pointed out that I had already got friends.

"So?" said Mum. "What's to stop you having another one?"

I said, "I don't want another one! You can't make yourself be friends with just *anybody*." Simply because their mum happened to have been in the hospital at the same time as yours.

Mum told me not to be such a grouch. "Don't be so unwelcoming! She's new, she doesn't know anyone. You're not shy! You could at least make a bit of an effort."

I could have, but I didn't. Me and Livy and Claire were quite happy as we were, just the three of us. We didn't need some little mouse tagging on! It wasn't till about a week later that Mum explained to me *why* Cupcake was so down. It was because she had a little brother who wasn't well and her mum and dad had just split up, and that was the reason she'd had to change schools, cos they couldn't afford to go on living where they were.

When I heard that I just felt *so sorry* for poor Cupcake. No wonder she was sad all the time! If my mum and dad split up, I would be sad all the time. More than just sad, I would be in floods of tears. I couldn't bear it!

It was thinking about her dad that made me start trying to be a bit nicer, like inviting her to join us at break time, and even, once, when Livy was away, going and sitting next to her. I didn't really think about her little brother all that much. I knew he couldn't walk too well, and that sometimes he fell over. I'd heard Mum say to Dad what a terrible shame it was, but it never occurred to me to ask what was wrong. It wasn't something Cupcake ever talked about. She seemed not to want to, and if she didn't want to then neither did I. I suppose I'm a bit of a coward in that way; I would rather not know.

In spite of making an effort to be more welcoming, I still didn't feel that Cupcake would ever really fit in and be one of us. I certainly never dreamt that we would end up best mates! It was her baby brother who brought us together. His name is Joey and he is the sweetest little boy I have ever known. Exactly how I would like my brother to be if ever I had one (instead of my spoilt brat of a sister, Rosie). He's so bright, and brave, and funny! He could still walk in those days, and even pedal about on his little tricycle. Sometimes his mum used to bring him with her when she came to pick up Cupcake from school. Other times, if he wasn't too well, she would leave him at home and the old lady who lives in the upstairs bit of their house would look after him.

"She doesn't mind," Cupcake assured me. "She loves Joey."

Everybody loves Joey! You can't not. Even if you are like me, and not at all a gooey sort of person, you still want to put your arms round him and give him a cuddle. He has these huge, dark eyes and curly hair and looks just so angelic! Whenever I say this, Cupcake goes "Huh! That's what you think," making like she finds him as big a pain as I find Rosie. But it is all put on. I was quite shocked the first time she said it, but now I realise it is important to her to pretend that he's no different from anyone else's little brother. In fact, he's full of mischief and manages to get up to all kinds of tricks, like the time he collected a load of slugs from the garden and put them in a dish on the kitchen table.

Cupcake *screeched*. I know, cos I was there! I just went, "Yeeeurgh!" but Cupcake shot out of her chair going, "Take them away, take them away! That's disgusting!"

In this hurt voice, Joey said he'd got them for us as a treat. He thought we'd enjoy them. He said that French people enjoyed them.

That really cracked me up. "That's *snails*!" I said. "Not slugs!"

Joey said, "Slugs is only snails without any shell." And then he picked up the bowl and ever so politely held it out to me. "You could try one!"

I said, "I don't think so."

"Just get rid of them!" screamed Cupcake.

Joey sighed and did his best to look hurt, but I knew he was only playacting cos he couldn't help this big, happy grin spreading across his face.

"See?" said Cupcake. "See what I mean? He does it on purpose!"

Joey tries ever so hard to behave the same as any normal little boy, only you can't say this to Cupcake cos it gets her really upset. I said it once, when I'd tried to help him on to his tricycle and he'd pushed me away and struggled on to it by himself. In this small, tight voice Cupcake said, "What d'you mean, the same as any normal little boy? He *is* a normal little boy. You saw what he did the other day!" She meant with the slugs. I knew that in spite of her screeching and saying how disgusting it was, she had been secretly quite pleased. Putting bowls of slugs on the kitchen table in the hope of making your sister feel sick is the sort of thing that little boys are supposed to get up to. To make her feel better I told her how *I* would like a brother like Joey – "Cos my sister is just sooo annoying!" – and that immediately made Cupcake stick up for Rosie, and we had a long discussion about whether or not she is spoilt. *Which she is.* Take my word for it! Cupcake said, "Yes, but she's only six years old." She said that Joey had been spoilt when he was six years old.

"And still is!" That was her mum, suddenly appearing through the back door. She said, "You two girls between you spoil that boy rotten."

I don't think we do! We just like to make him happy. We like to invent games that he can play, and read to him, and take him up the park. Once, for his birthday, we even wrote a special story for him. It was fifteen pages long, with pictures. We printed it out on the computer and made a proper cover so it looked like a real book that you could buy in a shop. It was called *Man on the Moon*. It was all about this boy who dreamt of becoming a spaceman only everybody told him he couldn't cos of being in a wheelchair. Then one day some aliens came from outer space and with the help of their advanced technology they turned the wheelchair into a spaceship, and the boy went whizzing off to the moon and it was all over the television, Wheelie Boy in Moon Trip.

Cupcake said, "Wheelie boys can do anything they want!"

Joey loved the book so much he read it to pieces and we had to print it out all over again. We thought about getting it published, except we couldn't decide which names to use. Our real names or our nicknames? We tried it both ways:

MAN ON THE MOON
by Fudge Cassidy & the Cupcake Kid

MAN ON THE MOON
by Danielle Cassidy & Lisa Costello

I thought we ought to use our real names, so as to sound more professional, like proper writers, but Cupcake said that would mean everybody would know who we were.

"They might even put our pictures in the local paper!"

Personally I would love to have my picture in the local paper. I would love everybody knowing who I am! But Cupcake's not into fame the way I am, and in the end we spent so much time arguing that we never did send the book to a publisher. Which I think is a pity, as it was really good, and we will probably never have the time to write another one. I wish now that I had given in and agreed to use our nicknames, in spite of them not being very professional. I bet the papers would still have found out who we were. I could have been a local celeb!

It was my dad who gave us the nicknames. He is quite a funny man, always making jokes. He laughed and laughed at the idea of me being Fudge Cassidy, though I would like to say right here and now that *I am not called Fudge because I'm a pudge*. And not because fudge does happen to be my all-time favourite treat. Well, practically my favourite *food*. I would live on fudge if I were allowed to! All kinds of fudge: chocolate fudge, vanilla fudge, cherry fudge. Even fudge with nuts in, though it is a bit of a drag having to pick the nuts out.

Dad was watching me do this one day, spitting out the nuts and gobbling up the fudge, and that is when he cried out "Fudge Cassidy!" like it was the best joke he had ever made. I suppose it's what's called a play on words. See, there's this movie called *Butch Cassidy & the Sundance Kid* that my dad is kind of obsessed with. He's got it on DVD and every year on his birthday he sits and watches it. (Like Mum with *The Sound of Music*.) I watched it with him one year, after he started calling me Fudge, but I couldn't get what he saw in it. It's about these two men who rob a bank and become outlaws and in the end they are shot, which is a bit sad I suppose, cos even though they are bank robbers they are not really bad people, and sometimes they are quite funny. I liked it when one of them rides round on a bicycle singing this song about raindrops. "Raindrops keep falling on my head." That is my favourite part!

I told Cupcake about it and taught her the song, and every now and then she'd jump on Joey's tricycle and ride round the garden singing it, except she used to change the words to "Cupcakes keep falling on my head". I know it sounds a bit childish, but Joey thought it was really funny. He thought it was even funnier when I changed the words to *fudge* keeps falling on my head. He used to squeal and go, "Eeeurgh, bird poo!" He was only little, after all. Well, seven years old. That is quite little.

Oh, I nearly forgot about Cupcake and how she became the Cupcake Kid. It was cos once when she came to tea and Mum had bought all these different coloured cupcakes – pink and lemon and strawberry and chocolate, plus some with sprinkles and some with little silver balls – Cupcake greedily went and ate one of each, which made six altogether. *Six cupcakes!* I have never let her forget it. Cupcake rather boastfully says, "And I wasn't even sick!" Dad was impressed. He said he had never seen anything like it, and that if I were Fudge Cassidy then she was obviously The Cupcake Kid. Which is what we have been ever since.

Mum says if we don't stop calling each other by our silly nicknames we'll live to regret it.

"Believe me," she says, "you won't want to be known as Fudge when you're my age!"

I expect that may be true, but it is way too far ahead for me to worry about it. In any case, Mum can't really say that our nicknames are silly; not now that we've lived up to them. Little did we know when Cupcake's mum took that photograph of us in the back garden, showing off our new school uniforms, that we were about to embark on a life of crime. That movie that Dad loves so much, the Butch Cassidy movie? It nearly came true. Me and Cupcake didn't exactly rob a bank, but for a short time we were handling stolen goods...

CHAPTER TWO

It was Cookie that got us started on our life of crime. Not that he was called Cookie back then. Back then he was just "the puppy". The puppy that lived in the garden over the wall.

See, at the back of our block of flats there's this old, crumbly wall that me and Cupcake used to use for tennis practice. We'd be out there whatever the weather, walloping about with our tennis racquets. Cupcake was never as keen as I was, but I can always get round her! All I had to do was wail, "You know how important it is to me!"

The reason it was so important was because I had this dream that one day, if I practised hard enough, I might end up a big star, playing at Wimbledon. I have a different dream now: I am going to be a TV celeb. I sort of gave up on Wimbledon; I got sick of losing tennis balls. It was mainly me who lost them, I have to admit. I am quite an energetic sort of player. I'd take a good *swipe*, and instead of bouncing off the wall the thing would go flying right over the top and into the garden on the other side. Well! You can't keep buying new tennis balls all the time, and you can't keep trailing all the way round the block and knocking on someone's door and asking "Please can we get our ball back?" Specially not when the person who answers the door is this crotchety old woman who complains that she is *trying* to watch television or *trying* to get a bit of rest. After the first few times Cupcake wouldn't come with me any more; it didn't matter how much I begged and pleaded. She said, "I can't! She's too horrible."

"She's only an old woman," I said.

"So you go and ask," said Cupcake.

I could have, I suppose; crotchety old women don't frighten *me*. But quite honestly it was getting to be a bit of a drag, especially when you went to all that trouble and then she wasn't there.

"Prob'ly be easiest if we just climbed over," I said.

Cupcake is such a scaredy-cat! She wouldn't do that, either. She whispered, "What if we got caught?"

I said, "We're not doing anything wrong! We're only getting our ball back."

"I dunno." Cupcake pressed the strings of her tennis racquet against her face, making her nose go all squashed. "It's still trespassing." Thing about Cupcake is she does have this tendency to dither. Me, I just go ahead and do things.

"Look, you stay here," I said. "I'll go. You keep a lookout."

That was when I took my first step towards a life of crime... I didn't realise it at the time, of course; I mean, what's a little bit of trespassing? No one was going to put me in prison for just climbing over a wall and getting my own property back. But I guess that's how it always is. You start off with small things like trespassing and before you know it you're a full-blown criminal.

It was quite easy hoisting myself up. I used an old bucket to stand on, then shoved my toes into cracks in the brickwork. Cupcake stood jittering while I swung myself over the top and jumped down on the other side. Almost before I'd even landed, a *thing* had launched itself at me. A furry, wriggling thing that made little squeaking noises. I went "Yow!" and fell in a heap with the furry thing on top of me. Next thing I know, Cupcake's peering over the top of the wall going, "Fudge? What's happening?" And then she saw the furry thing and went, "Oh!" And then, "*Oh!*" And then, "It's the puppy!"

We'd seen the puppy before; just quick glimpses when we'd knocked at the door. He'd be there, snuffling at the door crack, trying to say hello, and the old woman would always kick him back inside. She didn't kick to *hurt*, I don't think, cos she only wore slippers, but one time the puppy whimpered, like maybe he'd crashed into something. It didn't seem to me a very kind way to treat a little friendly animal. But then of course she didn't treat me and Cupcake very nicely, either, considering all we wanted was our ball back. It wasn't like we went round there on purpose to annoy her.

Cupcake's voice came squeaking anxiously over the wall at me. "Fudge? Are you OK?"

By this time I was flat on my back and the puppy was smothering me in a frenzy of wet kisses. I went, "Help! Ow! Ooch!" and promptly collapsed into giggles. Which is when Cupcake took *her* first step towards a life of crime. Before I knew it, she was over the wall and flying to my rescue. Maybe she *is* quite brave, after all! She said later that she thought I was being attacked.

Cupcake isn't used to dogs; in fact she is a bit scared of them. But not even Cupcake could be scared of a tiny puppy. Once she understood that he was just being friendly, and that the strange noises I was making were giggles, and not death rattles, she went all gooey and melty and wanted to cuddle him. But the puppy had other ideas. He was so pleased to have us in his garden! I'm sure he thought we'd climbed over the wall just to play with him. He immediately ran off and fetched a tennis ball – one of *our* tennis balls! – and came scampering back with it in his mouth. Plain as can be he was saying, "Throw it for me! Throw it for me!" So of course we did.

Cupcake got quite carried away! She just wouldn't stop. In the end I had to remind her that we were trampling about in someone else's garden.

"She could come out any minute!"

That got her moving. She shot back over the wall like she was jet-propelled, with me scrabbling after. And then, guess what? I realised that I'd gone and left the tennis ball behind!

Cupcake said, "Well, but we couldn't have taken it off him. It's his toy!"

I agreed; it would have been too heartless. We perched on the upturned bucket and peered over, watching as he went scampering off up the garden, throwing the ball in the air with his mouth and chasing after it.

"So *cute*," sighed Cupcake.

All puppies are cute. Much cuter than babies, *I* think, though of course that is only my opinion. But it was the first time Cupcake had ever properly met one, so naturally she thought he was special. She asked me what sort of breed he was. "Is he a pedigree?"

I said I didn't know. "He could just be a mongrel." I added that some people reckon mongrels are best. Cupcake shook her head.

"I think he's a pedigree," she said. She didn't know any more than I did! She didn't even know *as much* as I did. But it was obviously what she wanted to believe, so I didn't argue with her.

Now that we knew the puppy was there, we started taking quick peeps over the wall before getting on with our tennis practice. *My* tennis practice. Cupcake seemed to have got more interested in watching the puppy than helping me prepare for Wimbledon.

If he was in the garden by himself, without the old woman, we'd call to him and he'd come rushing up, all happy, tail wagging and ready for a game. Even I wasn't quite brave enough to climb over again, but we broke bits of stick off a nearby tree and threw them for him, and once we found an old burst football and lobbed that over, and he carried it off as proud as could be, shaking it from side to side.

Sometimes the old lady was out there, hanging washing on a clothes whizzy thing, or prodding about in the flower beds with a trowel. She never played with the puppy like we did. He tried so hard to make her! He used to run and fetch a toy and push it at her, or drop it by her side then back away with his bum in the air and his tail whirring in circles. *I* knew what he was saying. "Go on, missus! Throw it for us!"

But the old woman just ignored him. Either that or she shoved him out of the way. She really didn't seem to like him very much. Quite often she'd shout at him.

"Just stop *bothering* me!"

One time she whacked him for digging up one of her flowers. Poor little boy! He didn't know it was wrong. He was just trying to have fun. Another time we saw him in the garden by himself, tossing something small and bright into the air and catching it as it came down. Me and Cupcake were clapping and going "Yay!" and "Well done!" I suppose you could say we were encouraging him. Maybe we shouldn't have, cos all of a sudden the old woman came bursting out of the back door and started screeching.

"You bad dog! *Bad!* Drop that! Stop it! Drop it this instant!"

At first the puppy thought it was a game, he thought she was playing with him at last, but then he started to cower, and his ears went back and his tail crept between his legs, and the old lady grabbed the small, bright thing he'd been playing with and gave him a sharp crack across his nose. Oh, he did yelp! We felt so sorry for him. In a doubtful voice, afterwards, Cupcake said, "I suppose he has to learn." But you don't teach children by hitting them, so why teach puppies that way? We hated the old woman for that.

"I told you she was horrible," said Cupcake.

We still didn't know what the puppy's name was. The old woman never seemed to call him anything except "Bad dog". We just called him Boy. I was the one who came up with the name Cookie. We were perched on our bucket, dangling a pair of old woollen tights over the wall for the puppy to play with. I'd tied a big knot in one of the legs, and the puppy was tugging and making little growly noises.

"Thinks he's *sooo* clever," crooned Cupcake. "Such a *big grown-up* boy!"

She was getting to be like one of those yucky, show-off mums who are for ever going on about how wonderful their kids are. I tried teasing her about it, but instead of laughing – cos it *was* funny, well, I thought it was – she just hunched a shoulder and went "Humph." It wasn't like Cupcake; she usually has a good sense of humour. I can almost always make her laugh. But she'd been a bit down just lately. The puppy was the only thing that seemed to bring a smile to her face.

I said, "Here! You play with him." I thought it might cheer her up. She took one leg of the tights and obediently hung on to it, but not with very much enthusiasm. She'd suddenly gone all miserable and quiet. I did my best to make a game out of it. I said, "Grr!" and "Go for it!" and shook my head madly from side to side making growly noises, but the puppy could obviously sense there'd been a change of mood cos he dropped his knotted end and sat down instead to have a scratch.

I said, "Here, boy!" And then, "Know what?"

Cupcake said, "What?"

"We ought to call him Cookie."

There was a silence. I said, "The dog in Joey's book? He looks just like him!"

Cupcake sighed and said, "Mm… maybe."

"He does!"

Joey had this book, *Charlie Clark,* all about a little boy called Charlie and his dog, Cookie. Charlie and Cookie got up to all kinds of mischief. The book was one of Joey's favourites; almost as big a favourite as *Man on the Moon.* I don't know how many times he must have read it, but it always had him chuckling. He loved the idea of a boy and his dog having adventures. Maybe it's because *he*'d have liked to have adventures, same as all the tough little kids who lived in our block and were always getting into trouble for climbing on garage roofs or kicking footballs through windows or jamming the lifts by messing around with the buttons. Joey couldn't do any of those things – but Charlie could! So could Cookie. Charlie and Cookie went everywhere together. And in spite of Cupcake and her "Mm... maybe," our puppy looked just like Cookie's twin. Brown and white and cheeky.

That was when I had my great idea – well, I thought it was a great idea. Why didn't Cupcake ask her mum if *they* could have a dog?

"For Joey," I said. "Joey would love it!"

Know what? All she did was grunt. Like, *hmm*.

"I'm thinking of Joey," I said.

She didn't say anything at all to that. I felt like shaking her. I said, "*Well?*"

"Well, what?" said Cupcake.

"Why not try asking her?"

"I'm not asking my mum if we can have a dog! She's got enough to do, looking after Joey."

"But it would make him so happy!" I said.

"How?" She suddenly turned on me. "How would it

make him happy? He couldn't play with it, he couldn't take it out for walks, he c—"

"We'd take it out!"

"*And that would make him happy?*" She didn't have to bite my head off. "How d'you know what'd make him happy? He's not your brother!"

That really got to me. "Doesn't mean I don't care about him!" I said.

She obviously felt a bit ashamed, then. She mumbled something about being sorry, but that it wasn't like I was responsible for him. I said, "No, but I still don't like it when he's sad."

She muttered, "I expect you'd be sad if you were in a wheelchair."

If I was in a wheelchair I'd be so frustrated I would probably scream and smash things. But Joey was such a bright, sunny little boy! He'd always just seemed to accept that there were certain things he couldn't do. Until I'd gone round the previous weekend I'd never known him to be grumpy. Cupcake had been riding round the garden on Joey's tricycle singing her silly cupcake song, but for once he hadn't shown any interest. Usually he demanded that I do "the bird poo one". I did offer. I said, "Come on! Let's do it together… you get on the bike and I'll push you, and we'll both sing. *Fudge keeps a-falling on my head…* "

But he wouldn't. I grabbed his hand and tried to coax him, but he just snatched his hand away and shouted, "Don't wanna!" I was really upset. Now Cupcake was upsetting me as well!

I said, "Look, I'm just saying… if he had a dog he mightn't mind so much about—"

"What?" she said. "About what?"

"About…" I faltered. She'd sounded really fierce. I wasn't used to Cupcake sounding fierce. "Being in a wheelchair?" I whispered.

Cupcake's face had gone bright red. "Why don't you just shut up?" She hissed it at me. "You don't know what you're talking about!"

What had I done to deserve that? She was in a really

weird mood. I hated to quarrel with her, but you can't just let yourself be trampled on. I said, "OK, if that's the way you want it. Sorry I bothered." And then I walked off, swishing my tennis racquet and leaving her there to sulk.

It was the first time me and Cupcake had ever seriously fallen out. And I still didn't know what it was I had done to upset her!

In school next day we didn't seem to be talking. Instead of sitting next to each other like we usually did, we both deliberately chose seats next to other people. Everybody noticed. At lunch time we even ended up at different tables. Livy said, "What's going on?"

I said, "Nothing. Why?"

"Just asking," said Livy.

I gave her this stony glare, and she pulled a face and said, "Well, pardon me for breathing!" and began to talk to someone else.

Me and Cupcake caught each other's eye and quickly looked away again. I think we both felt a bit foolish. And upset, too. I can always tell when Cupcake is upset. She droops, and sags, and goes very quiet. I tend to do the exact opposite. I get all busy and **LOUD**, and charge about yelling and making jokes in the hope that no one will notice. I did a *lot* of charging about and yelling that particular day. In art, I charged about so much I managed to upset the fruit and flower arrangement we were supposed to be painting and skidded halfway across the studio on a bunch of grapes. Mrs Rae, who is normally very relaxed, threatened to send me out if I didn't control myself.

"What's the matter with you, Danielle? You're completely hyperactive!"

Next day, it was like nothing had ever happened. Like both of us had decided the time had come to make up. We didn't actually *say* anything, but Cupcake came and sat next to me, same as usual, and asked me how I'd got on with the French translation we'd been given for homework. When I said that I hadn't got beyond the first few words, she said, "D'you want to borrow mine?" and slid her book across the desk for me to look at. It was like a sort of peace offering. Like in her own way she was saying sorry for having been so mean and grouchy. It immediately made me feel that I wanted to say sorry, too, so I thanked her and promised "I won't actually *copy.*"

Cupcake said, "You can if you want. I don't mind." Which was really generous of her, since she nearly always gets an A in French, whereas I am totally hopeless and usually get a big red D, plus rude comments along the lines of "*Danielle, I really would appreciate it if you made a bit of an effort to stay awake when I am teaching you.*" But anyway I didn't totally copy as it might have got us into trouble. I am used to being in trouble, but it wouldn't have been fair on Cupcake.

After that, we were back to normal. I still had this feeling that Cupcake was a bit down, but sometimes with her it is hard to tell as she is naturally a quiet sort of person. She's also quite secretive. I tend to blurt everything out, whereas Cupcake keeps things to herself. Still, I didn't want to upset her again, so I did my best to pretend I hadn't noticed. I thought if I talked loudly enough it would act as a sort of cover and nobody else would notice, either, which I don't think they did. They are used to me being noisy and Cupcake being quiet.

Saturday morning I went round to her place, same as always. We liked to give Joey a bit of time before we went off to mooch round the shops or practise my tennis. He was really on form that morning! All bright and bubbly and wanting to do things. We took him into the garden and he insisted on trying to get on his tricycle without any help from me or Cupcake. Unfortunately he couldn't quite manage it, and toppled over on to the grass. We rushed to pick him up, but he pushed us away, going, "I can do it, I can do it!"

It is very difficult to just stand by and watch, but we knew we had to let him. He almost made it. Slowly he pulled himself back on to his feet, muttering, "Now I

fall *down*, now I get *up*. Now I fall *down*… now I get *up*!"
And then, at last, he let us help him.

We both hugged him, which was something we wouldn't have dared do a week ago. He'd been so angry the previous Saturday he'd probably have punched us. Now he was all cheeky and grinning and demanding the bird poo song as we pulled him round the garden on his bike.

We played for about an hour, until it was time for Joey to rest. I said to Cupcake, "Let's go and see if Cookie's there!"

He was, but so was the old woman, so we didn't like to call to him. We just perched on our bucket and watched for a while as he pottered about the garden. His legs were still rubbery, and while he was digging in a bit of old earth, one of them suddenly gave way and he sat down with a thump, looking quite surprised. I immediately thought of Joey; *his* legs kept giving way. It was what had happened that morning, when he'd tried to get on his bike. Now I fall *down*, now I get *up*.

Impulsively, as we stepped off the bucket, I said, "Joey seems so much happier! D'you think he's getting better?"

Cupcake didn't say anything. She just frowned, and dug the tip of her trainer into a bit of soft earth at the bottom of the wall.

"I mean... he almost managed to get on his bike by himself!"

In this small, tight voice Cupcake said, "This time last year he *could* get on his bike by himself."

"Well... y-yes. But he's better than he has been!"

"Last year," said Cupcake, "he could still ride round the garden. When we first came here, he could still walk."

I fell silent, chewing on my lip. I could remember Joey walking. He used to come with Mrs Costello to pick Cupcake up from school.

"He just gets worse all the time," she cried. "He's not *ever* going to get better!"

And then she burst into tears and I didn't know

what to say. I felt that I should do something, like put my arms round her or something, but I just stood there, staring at the ground and twiddling my tennis racquet.

After a bit I managed to mumble that I was sorry.

"It's all right. It's not your fault." Cupcake wiped her nose on the back of her hand. "You weren't to know."

But I should have done! I'd watched Joey grow weaker and weaker and I'd never once asked any questions. I'd tried telling myself it was because of not liking to think about people being ill, but maybe it was simply because I was scared of what the answer might be. The truth is, I hadn't really wanted to know.

"I should have told you," said Cupcake. She said that she had always known, right from the beginning. Her mum had never kept any secrets from her. "I'm sorry! It's just – " the tears came welling up again – "I couldn't bring myself to talk about it!"

I pulled a crumpled tissue from my pocket and silently handed it to her. Then I patted her on the back a few times, like I'd seen people do in movies when they were trying to comfort someone. I felt really ashamed of being so useless. I'm not usually so useless! If Cupcake had fallen off a cliff I would be the first one scrambling down to save her. If she were to fall into the canal I would dive straight in after her, never mind that I can't swim. If she got sucked into a bog I would tear off the branch of a nearby tree and push it out to her, and wouldn't let go no matter how close I came to being sucked in with her. But now, because she was crying, I couldn't think of a single thing to do except just stand helplessly by and watch.

After a while she dried her eyes and blew her nose and said again that she was sorry.

"Want to play some tennis?" I asked.

We played for a bit, but not for very long. It suddenly seemed kind of pointless, bashing tennis balls against a wall when Cupcake was so sad. We didn't go and look round the shops, either; I didn't even suggest it.

"Think I'll go home now," said Cupcake.

She didn't ask me to go with her, but I understood.

"See you tomorrow," I said.

Cupcake just nodded, and ran off.

CHAPTER THREE

Mum was surprised to see me back so soon.

"I thought you were out there training for Wimbledon?"

It was her idea of a joke. Danielle training for Wimbledon, ha ha! Mum always treats my ambitions as a joke, it doesn't matter what they are. She thinks my present ambition, to be a TV celeb, is the biggest joke ever. She says, "Surely celebs have to *do* something?"

I will do something! It's just I haven't yet decided what.

Rather sternly I said, "Cupcake had to go home."

"Oh. Well! In that case, if you're at a loose end," said Mum, "maybe you could entertain Rosie."

I didn't want to entertain Rosie.

"I wish you would," said Mum. "She's feeling a bit sorry for herself."

Just because she had the sniffles. Not even a proper cold! And there was poor little Joey, stuck in a wheelchair and still managing to laugh.

"Go on," said Mum. "Do something nice for once!"

I said, "I don't feel like it."

"Why? What's wrong?"

"Cupcake said Joey isn't going to get any better!" I blurted out. "She said he's only going to get worse!"

"Oh." Mum stopped what she was doing, which was chopping stuff for dinner. She wiped her hands on her apron and held them out to me. "Oh, sweetheart, I'm so sorry!"

I used to have lots of cuddles with Mum when I was little, until Rosie came along. Not that I cared. I was too old for all that kind of stuff in any case. But just now and then, like when *she* isn't around, we have a bit of a secret snuggle. It can be quite a comfort.

"Is that why you're back early?" said Mum.

I nodded, with my head pressed into the bib of her apron, which smelt for some reason of oranges. Now I always think of oranges when I think of Joey. I expect I always will.

"It's not true, is it?" I whispered. "He won't just go on getting worse?"

Mum knows how much I love that little boy. She made me sit down with her at the kitchen table, and explained to me how Joey had this condition that made his muscles weak. She told me that what Cupcake had said was true: Joey wouldn't ever get any better. He would just slowly get worse. I cried, then, like Cupcake had cried. I was still crying when Rosie came into the kitchen whining that she was bored. For once, Mum sent her packing.

"Not now, Rosie! I'm talking to your sister."

She's not used to being spoken to like that. She went into this massive sulk and curled up on the sofa sucking her thumb like a stupid baby. Thankfully, Mum didn't suggest I might like to entertain her. Instead, she took a £5 note out of her purse and told me to "Go and buy something to cheer yourself up."

It's the funny thing about my mum. She is one of those people who can either be totally unreasonable – like the time I accidentally set fire to my bedroom curtains and she started yelling and bawling and going completely raving berserk like I'd purposely run at them with a lighted match – or she can be, quite simply, THE BEST.

I immediately rushed down to the shops to find something for Joey. I spent ages dithering about like Cupcake, unable to decide whether to get him a *boy* thing, like an Action Man or a Star Wars figure, or a boy/girl thing, like a soft toy. I thought maybe a soft toy that he could cuddle. First I picked up a fluffy bunny, and then I picked up a woolly frog, and then I put the frog back and picked up a tiger. And then I put *that* back and picked up the frog again. I just couldn't make up my mind. I thought how awful it must be to be Cup, and to live like that the whole time. I was driving myself mad!

And then I saw it... a tiny little dog, like a miniature Cookie. It was only a few centimetres high, but it was brown and white with big, flappy ears, just like Cookie. It also cost *more than Mum had given me*, but I didn't mind. I still had my pocket money, which I'd probably only have spent on sweets.

When I got home, Rosie was full of her usual nauseating bounce.

"What have you got there?" she said.

I told her it was none of her business. "It's a present for someone far nicer than you!"

"I suppose it's for *Joey*," she said.

I said, "Yes, cos he deserves it!"

"Just cos he's in a *wheel*chair."

There are times when I really *would* like to hit her. If I believed in violence, which I don't. But sometimes you can just about be driven to it.

"I saw you crying earlier," she said. "What were you crying about?"

I said, "I wasn't crying. You just shut up!"

She immediately started screeching. "I'll tell Mum you said that!"

At that point Mum came in and asked rather wearily what was going on.

"She told me to shut up!" screeched Rosie.

I said, "Yes, cos she was sticking her nose in where it doesn't belong!"

Later, Mum told me that I shouldn't be too hard on my dear little sister. She said, "Sometimes I think she feels a bit jealous."

I said, "*Jealous?* What of?"

"The way you make it seem that you love Joey more than you love her," said Mum. "I know he's a very sweet little boy, but Rosie is your sister!"

I was gobsmacked when Mum said that. If anyone was going to be jealous I'd have thought it should be me, considering how Mum always *always* took Rosie's side.

When Dad got back from football, happy cos for once his team had won, she hurled herself at him going, "Daddy, Daddy!" in this silly little voice that grown-ups seem to find cute. Dad said, "Hey! How's my little one?" and picked her up and tossed her about and started tickling her. Totally sick-making. "Feeling any better, Babyface?"

And then he remembered that he had another daughter, and turned to me and ruffled my hair and said, "And how about old Fudgekins here? No need to ask how she is. Tough as old boots, this one!"

You see what I mean? One of us is *spoilt and pampered*, the other is tough as old boots. Well, OK!

That suits me. I might have had a bit of a cry in the kitchen earlier on, but it wasn't the sort of thing I do every day. When Dad came up to me later and put his arm round me, he said, "Sorry, Fudgekins! Mum told me you've been a bit upset." I just shook my head and muttered, "I'm all right."

"About Joey..." Dad sat down next to me on the sofa and tried to pull me close, but I made myself go stiff, like a board. *I did not want to cry.* Crying makes your head ache. It also makes your eyes go red. I didn't want Rosie to see me like that.

"Fudgekins? I know it's unfair," said Dad, "especially when he's hardly any older than Rosie, but it's a sad fact of life that these things happen. At least he has a mum and a sister who love him, which lots of kids don't have."

My eyes were starting to prick. I wished Dad would just go away!

"You love him, too, don't you?" said Dad. "See, in some ways he's a very lucky little boy."

★ 55 ☆

I thought, *Dad, how can you say that?* I swallowed very hard. Any minute now, I'd be in floods of tears.

That was when Rosie came prancing in. *Again.* But for once I was actually glad to see her. I immediately jumped up, going, "I just remembered! I've got homework to do!" and rushed down the passage to my bedroom.

I did actually do some homework. It was only boring geography, but at least it took my mind off things.

Next day, I whizzed round to give Joey his present.

"See? Look! A tiny little Cookie!"

His face lit up and he stretched his hands out eagerly. His mum said, "Joey! What do you say?"

He obediently told me "A big *THANK YOU!*"

"And give Dani a kiss?"

"Give Dani a *BIG* kiss!"

And he did, too, reaching out with both arms and hooking them round my neck.

"Thank you, thank you!"

It seems very odd to me, that a little boy who has so many problems should be so easy to please, while Rosie does nothing but whinge and complain. *She* wouldn't be content with anything less than the latest mobile phone or a flat-screen telly. She actually asked Mum the other day if she could have an ipod for her birthday. "For when I'm seven." What does *she* want with an ipod??? I don't expect Joey even knows what an ipod is. Unlike Rosie, who thinks she's just *so* smart and *so* sophisticated, Joey is still just a little boy. Rosie likes to pretend she's six-going-on-sixteen, but Joey is more like an innocent five-year-old. It's not that he's slow, just that he's never had a chance to get streetwise. That's all.

Anyway, we went into the garden, same as usual, and Joey insisted on taking Cookie for a ride on his bike. Cupcake said, "Why don't we make a collar and lead for him? Then you could ride and he could walk."

Joey liked that.

"I'll go and do it," said Cupcake.

It was while she was indoors, making the collar and lead, that I had my bright idea: we could take Joey to see the *real* Cookie. I suggested it to Cupcake, and she said, "Oh! Yes. He'd love that!" We had to check first with Mrs Costello that it would be OK. Naturally, we didn't tell her about climbing over the wall to get tennis balls back, we just said there was this adorable little puppy that looked like Cookie. Mrs Costello said all right, so long as we were back by midday, and we set off triumphantly with Joey in his wheelchair, still clutching his new toy.

"We're going to see a *real* Cookie," I told him.

Well! I really do think it was one of the very best ideas I've ever had. I think Cupcake would agree with me. She doesn't always approve of my ideas as sometimes in the past they have got us into trouble, like when I decided to give us both a fake tattoo and our arms swelled up and we had to have antibiotics. Our mums were quite cross, and so was Cupcake, as antibiotics make her tummy go funny. But even she said that watching Cookie chasing round the garden was the best treat Joey had had since coming to see me in our school play at Christmas. He was, like, *transfixed*. We stood him up on the seat of his wheelchair, with me on one side and Cupcake on the other, supporting him. I was on the bucket, and Cupcake was on an old car tyre we'd lugged over. It wasn't as high as the bucket, but she's taller than me so she could still see OK.

We couldn't call out to Cookie that day as the old woman was out there, sitting at a table drinking coffee. Cookie was doing his usual doggy stuff, digging up bits of garden, tugging at plants, chewing at what looked like one of our tennis balls. Joey got really excited. He kept squealing, and holding up his new toy going, "Cookie! Cookie!" We had to shush him in case the old woman came crosspatching up the garden and told us off. By the time we took him home he was obviously exhausted, cos of standing for so long, but he was still talking excitedly about Cookie.

Mrs Costello said, "Well, I can see you've had a good time!"

After that, of course, he wanted to come with us every day. What with wheeling him there, then wheeling him back, it meant I wasn't getting as much tennis practice as I should have done, but I was already beginning to wonder if perhaps I wasn't really cut out for life as an international tennis star, so I didn't really mind. In any case, making a little boy happy was far more important.

One day, when we were watching Cookie dig a hole at the foot of a prickly shrub, we saw his back leg give way again so that he sat down, with a flump, on his bottom. Joey chuckled happily. He said that Cookie was like him.

"Now he fall *down*, now he get *up*."

Another day, he was chasing to and fro in the middle of the garden, tossing something small and bright and shiny into the air and catching it again. Last time he had done that, the old woman had come running out in a rage and whacked him. This time, she obviously hadn't noticed.

"Serves her right," said Cupcake.

And then it happened: our *second* step towards a life of crime. It was Saturday morning, just one week after Cupcake had told me about Joey and I had gone home and cried all over Mum. We'd got Joey standing on the seat of his wheelchair, and we'd scrambled up beside him, but the garden was empty. No sign of Cookie.

"Looks like he's indoors," I said. "Want to go for a walk round the park, instead?"

"You can see lots of dogs there," said Cupcake.

But Joey fiercely shook his head and said *no.* "Wanna see Cookie!"

It got kind of boring, just standing there, staring at nothing. I was about to suggest the park again when the back door was suddenly flung open and Cookie came hurtling through the air, straight into the side of a big stone flower tub, *wham.* We heard the old woman's voice screaming after him: "You get out there and you stay out there!" With that, she slammed the door shut.

There was a startled silence, then Cupcake said, "She threw him!"

We watched, in a kind of frozen horror, as Cookie staggered to his feet. He wobbled a bit, and seemed dazed.

"She's hurt him," I said. "He's got concussion!"

Joey was almost beside himself. He kept wailing, "Why she do it? Why she hurt him?"

"Cos she's a mean, hateful old woman," said Cupcake. "She's not fit to have a dog!"

Joey was becoming quite distressed. He can't bear any kind of violence; even cartoons on the television upset him. He begged us to go and see if Cookie was all right. Me and Cupcake exchanged glances.

"Could go and knock at the door," I said.

"No!" Joey battered at me angrily. "Go inna *garden*!"

I said, "But it's not ours."

"Go inna garden!"

"It's all right," said Cupcake. "I'll go."

Before I could stop her, she had hoicked one leg over the wall and was jumping down on the other side. I couldn't believe it! *I* was the one who was supposed to be bold and fearless. Cupcake was the timid one. But there she was, halfway down the garden, crouched behind a prickly bush, calling to Cookie.

His ears flattened. Very slowly he began to crawl towards her, close to the ground, his tail at half-mast, but wagging ever so slightly. As soon as he reached her, Cupcake gathered him into her arms and came racing back to the wall. I said, "Is he OK?"

"I think so." Cupcake set him on the ground and he immediately jumped up at her, clutching at one of her legs with his front paws, plainly asking to be picked up again.

"Gimme, gimme!" Joey was holding out both arms, leaning so far forward I was scared he was going to fall.

I tried pulling him back, but he screamed and pushed me away. "Gimme, gimme!"

I knew I had to be firm. When Joey is frustrated, he tends to just lash out, which personally I can understand. I wasn't scared of him hitting me, but I didn't want him toppling headfirst over the wall and getting hurt.

"Joey, stop it," I said. "Sit down. If you sit down... we'll let you cuddle him!"

Cupcake said, "What?"

"It's all right, it's all right," I said, "just for a few minutes, then we'll put him back."

Now we were seriously embarking on a life of crime. Not only was Cupcake trespassing in someone's garden, she was abducting someone's puppy. *And I was aiding and abetting her.* You can be done for aiding and abetting. But I didn't care, it was worth it! Joey sat in his chair beaming, with Cookie in his arms, squirming and wriggling and covering his face in wet doggy kisses. Cupcake hung over the wall, watching, with this soppy smile on her face. I was still perched on my bucket, and I expect I had a soppy smile, as well. I mean, it was *really* touching! You would have had to have a heart of stone not to be moved by it.

I guess the old woman had a heart of stone. She took us by surprise; this voice suddenly came snarling at us.

"*What* do you think you are doing in my garden? And where is my dog?"

Cupcake slid back down with a frightened squeak. The old woman's head appeared over the wall. She looked at Joey cuddling Cookie, and her lips didn't even twitch.

"I'm waiting for an explanation," she said.

I opened my mouth to say that I was sorry, but Cupcake got in first. "We saw you throw him! You *hurt* him. You're always hurting him! You hit him and you kick him, and he's only a poor little puppy. How does he know he's not supposed to eat your mouldy flowers? You don't have to *hit* him!"

Cupcake was really going for it. I was desperate to add something of my own, but all I could think of to say was, "You should be reported!"

"Yes," said the old woman, "and so should you. You can think yourselves lucky if I don't go to the police. Now, give me that dog back and get out of my garden!"

It didn't seem that we had much choice. Slowly, Cupcake heaved herself over to our side of the wall. I reached down to take Cookie. I said, "Joey, let me have him... *please*."

"*No!*" With one hand he clutched Cookie; with the other, he did his best to fight me off. I could quite easily have plucked Cookie away from him, but it didn't seem fair to fight a handicapped little boy.

"He doesn't want to give him back," I said. "He's scared you'll hurt him again."

Joey clutched Cookie even tighter. "Not having him, not having him!" His voice rose to a scream. Cupcake said, "Joey!"

"*Not having him!*"

"Oh, for goodness' sake!" The old woman threw up her arms. "All this fuss over a mere dog. If you want it that badly, then take it!"

Pardon me??? Was she *serious*?

"Take it, take it! Just get it out of my sight!"

I glanced nervously at Cupcake. Her eyes had gone like flying saucers. I had this feeling that my mouth was dropping open. People don't just give their dogs to total strangers! Do they?

"Well, go on!" The old woman made an impatient shoo-ing motion with her hands. "What are you waiting for? Do you want it, or not?"

I cried, "Yes!" and spun Joey's wheelchair round before she could change her mind. Cupcake joined me, and all three of us, with Cookie still clutched in Joey's arms, went galloping off. The old woman's voice came shouting after us: "And don't ever let me catch you in my garden again!"

Cupcake's mum was a bit startled to see us arrive back home with a puppy. "What's this?" she said.

Me and Cupcake instantly broke into a mad kind of burble.

"There's this old woman—"

"In the garden—"

"Her garden—"

"Near the flats—"

"By the wall—"

"Slow down, slow down!" said Mrs Costello. "One of you – Lisa! Where did you get the dog from?"

"Puppy," said Cupcake. "He's a puppy!"

"All right, then, puppy! Where did you get it from?"

Cupcake poured it all out, telling her mum everything: how cruel the old woman was, and how it had upset Joey, and how he loved the puppy because he was like Cookie in his *Charlie Clark* book, and how he didn't want to give him back, so the old woman had said we could have him. "And please, Mum, *can* we?"

I could tell that her mum wasn't mad keen, but unlike the old woman Cupcake's mum has a heart made of marshmallow, especially where Joey's concerned. She took one look at him cuddling Cookie and shook her head in despair.

"I'll have to go and check," she said. "Make sure she really means it. I don't want to be accused of dognapping. One of you had better come with me in case I need to hear both sides of the story. Danielle?"

"No, I'll come!" Cupcake leapt forward, so I said I would stay and keep an eye on Joey. It seemed only fair to let Cupcake go, if that was what she wanted. After all, she had been the really brave one.

It was quite tense, waiting for Cupcake and her mum to come back. What if that mean old woman had changed her mind? Joey was so happy! And so was Cookie. Who could bear to part them?

Fortunately, we didn't have to wait long. Cupcake rushed into the kitchen, waving a lead and a dog bowl, followed by her mum, still shaking her head.

"So, it looks like we've got ourselves a puppy." She said that the puppy had been a present from the old woman's daughter. "A very silly present... she's far too old to cope. I think she was actually quite relieved to get rid of it."

Cupcake said, "*Him*. Not it." And then she turned to me, very proudly, and said, "He's a Beadle."

I said, "What's a Beadle?"

"It's his breed… a *Beadle*. I told you he was a pedigree!"

It turned out she meant Beagle. I typed it into Google and found a whole site devoted to them, with lots of pictures of adorable little patchwork puppies with long, flappy ears. Just like Cookie!

CHAPTER FOUR

Monday morning, at break, Cupcake went round telling everyone about Cookie.

"We've got this puppy. He's so cute! He belonged to this horrible old woman who was mean to him. She used to *kick* him. Didn't she?" She turned to me, but before I could open my mouth, or even just nod, she'd gone rattling on again. "Can you imagine? A tiny puppy? And one time she hit him. Like really hard, right across his nose."

"So what happened?" said Claire. "How'd you end up with him?"

"We threatened to report her and she got scared. Didn't she? She got really scared!"

I said, "Y—"

"She told us if we wanted him, we could take him. So now he's ours!"

"What sort is he?" said Livy. "Is he anything special?"

"Yes!" Cupcake smiled proudly. "He's a Beadle!"

I said, "*Beagle.*" Not that anybody took any notice. They were all too busy saying how they'd got Jack Russells or Labradors or springer spaniels. Someone then asked what a Beadle was. I tried again, I said, "*Beagle,*" as loudly as I could, but Cupcake just shouted right over the top of me.

"They're brown and white and about *this* size!"

It was unlike Cupcake to be so rude, but I forgave

her. She was obviously excited. She told me later that her mum had said getting Cookie was the best thing that had ever happened.

"He and Joey have just, like, totally bonded!" She said that Cookie wouldn't leave Joey's side; he even slept on his bed at night. She said, "Mum was a bit worried at first. She thought she had enough to cope with without having a puppy to look after, but I told her, we'd look after him! We'd take him for walks. We'd go up the park, and take Joey as well. We could do that OK, couldn't we?"

I didn't remind her that I had been the one who originally suggested it. I'd never seen her so happy. If she wanted to think it was her idea, that was OK by me.

Cupcake's mum had started to bring Joey after school, in his wheelchair, to meet Cupcake, and now Cookie came with them, trotting along on his lead at the side of the chair, as good as gold. When they reached the school gates and we all started pouring out, he would jump on to Joey's lap and sit there, with everyone going "Aaah! Sweet!" as they walked past. Joey kept telling people, "My dog, Cookie!" Soon, the whole of our year group knew about Joey and Cookie. So did lots of others. Even Year 12s would sometimes stop and say hello. Even, once, this really tough boy called Mason Brewster who I'd always thought was just a bully. He said, "Nice dog!" and gave Joey the thumbs up.

"He's a Beadle," said Cupcake. I'd given up trying to correct her.

Mum said to me that Cookie had done wonders for Joey. "It's really perked him up, poor little soul. He's had such a rough deal. That little dog has given him a new lease of life."

Joey and Cookie had become like me and Cupcake: inseparable. They just wouldn't be parted! One day cos it was wet Cupcake's mum said me and Cupcake had better take Cookie out on his own while Joey stayed behind, only guess what? Cookie wouldn't come! He kept running back to Joey and bark, bark, barking, until in the end Mrs Costello gave in and we wrapped Joey up and all went round the park together in the pouring rain.

Sometimes, we noticed, Cookie would run along on three legs, keeping one of his back legs off the ground. We mentioned it to Cupcake's mum and she said maybe he'd pulled a muscle from all the jumping he did. He was for ever bouncing up and down, like he was on springs. Bounce! on to Joey's lap. Bounce! on to the bed. Bounce! on to the table. I told one of my nans about it – my doggy nan, who has a Yorkshire terrier called Biscuit – and she said best to exercise him gently for the next few days and not let him race around too much, so we kept him on the lead, which he hated. We hated it, too, cos it wasn't any fun just walking slowly. Cookie wanted to run and play, and so did we! Even Joey liked to throw his ball for him. He said it wasn't fair, him not being allowed to play. He seemed to accept that *he* couldn't play; but it really upset him that Cookie couldn't.

I tried to explain. I said, "If he keeps rushing about, his leg won't ever get better."

"And then he won't ever be able to play," said Cupcake.

"He be like me," said Joey.

Me and Cupcake didn't know what to say to that. Fortunately, Joey said it for us. "Don't want Cookie be like me!" So after that he was the one telling Cookie to walk nicely, not run, and we waited anxiously for signs of improvement. But instead of getting better he just got worse! Soon he wasn't using his one leg at all, and it was obvious he was in pain cos now and then he yelped. In the end Cupcake's mum said she would have to take him to the vet.

She came to meet Cupcake from school that afternoon, as usual, with Joey and Cookie.

"How is he?" demanded Cupcake. "What did the vet say?"

Her mum said that the vet had given him some tablets to take.

"And that will make his leg all right?"

"We hope so," said her mum. "If not – well! We shall have to wait and see. Let's not anticipate the worst."

Alarm bells started to ring when she said that. Me and Cupcake shot worried glances at each other. In a quavery voice Cupcake said, "What would the worst be?"

"He might need to have an operation," said her mum.

Oh! Was that all?

"An operation isn't anything," I said. "My nan's had lots of operations."

"It wouldn't be very nice for him," said Cupcake.

"No, but if it made him better – it *would* make him better, wouldn't it?" I said.

Cup's mum agreed that it would. "But let's just hope it doesn't come to that. With any luck, the tablets will do the trick."

It was such a game, giving those tablets to Cookie! He was really cunning. To begin with, Cupcake's mum tried putting them in his food, but he always managed to suss them out, so in the end we had to push them down his throat – and even then he sometimes had this clever trick of hiding them in the side of his mouth and trying to bury them under the sofa cushions when he thought no one was looking. I was the best one at giving them to him! Cupcake was scared she was going to hurt him, and her mum said that her hands were too big to go into such a tiny mouth. Cupcake said, "Fudge can do it! She knows about dogs." So I rang my doggy nan and she told me to push them *right* down his throat, then hold his muzzle and massage under his chin. "That'll make him swallow!"

Nan was right. I got him to swallow every time! I do have a way with dogs. Well, all animals, really. I once reared some frogspawn until it turned into tadpoles. Not everyone can do that; Cupcake's frogspawn went all mouldy and never even hatched. Maybe that's what I'll be famous for! I don't mean rearing tadpoles, but having a way with animals. Danielle Cassidy, Animal Supremo!

For ten whole days Cookie took his tablets, and we waited eagerly to see if he stopped limping, but he didn't. If anything, he limped worse than he had before. The next step, according to the vet, was an X-ray. Cupcake wailed, "He'll hate it!"

"An X-ray's nothing," I said. "I've had X-rays. I've had two! They don't hurt."

"No, but he'll have to have an anaesthetic," said Cupcake.

"Anaesthetic isn't anything," I said. "My nan's had loads."

I was just trying to cheer her up. The littlest thing can send her into a fit of the glooms. I told her that we needed to be *strong.*

"We don't want Joey being upset."

"He already is," said Cupcake dismally. "He asked Mum last night if Cookie was going to die."

I said, "*Die?* Of course he's not going to die!"

"Well, *I* know that," said Cupcake, though she didn't sound as if she did. She sounded like someone who'd just walked into the garden and seen a big sign saying **THE END OF THE WORLD IS NIGH.** "Joey's so little," she said, "he doesn't understand!"

"That's why we have to be strong," I said.

I decided that I would have to be strong for both of us. Cupcake is one of those people, she always expects bad things to happen. Me, I always look on the bright side! Dad says I'm an incurable optimist.

The day of Cookie's X-ray, Cupcake's mum didn't bring Joey to meet Cupcake from school as they were fetching Cookie from the vet. I went back with Cupcake to find Cookie cuddling on Joey's lap. He was still a bit groggy, but he looked up and wagged his stumpy tail at us. Cupcake's mum said, "I'm glad you're here, Dani. We have to talk, and you're almost part of the family."

I really liked that she said that! But I wasn't sure I

liked that we had to talk. It didn't sound good. Cupcake whispered, "Is it about Cookie?"

Her mum said yes, it was. The vet had confirmed that he needed an operation. "And please, Dani, don't say an operation is nothing!"

"No, don't!" cried Cupcake.

"It's not the operation itself," said her mum. "It's a question of being able to afford it... Girls, it's going to cost nearly £300! I just don't have that kind of money."

We were both shocked into silence. I hadn't ever thought about the money, and I don't think Cupcake had, either. We both gazed across at Cookie, innocently snuggled up on Joey's lap.

"Cookie's not going have operation?" said Joey. His lower lip was trembling. "He's not going get better?"

"It's all right; he'll still be able to walk!" I said. "Just on three legs. That's all!"

"Yes, he could do that," said Cupcake. "He could manage OK on three legs. Couldn't he, Mum?"

Her mum shook her head. "That would be cruel. His bad leg would always hurt him, and what if he damaged another one? He really does need the operation. But I simply can't afford it!"

So what was she saying?

"The kindest thing would be to ask an animal shelter to take him, then maybe they could find someone willing to give him a home and pay for his treatment."

"Mum, no!" shrieked Cupcake. "We can't give Cookie away!"

"I don't want to," said her mum, "believe me! I just can't see any alternative. Maybe — " she looked hopefully at Joey — "maybe we could take another dog from the animal shelter in his place?"

"No!" Joey clutched protectively at Cookie. "Don't want another dog! I want Cookie!"

"But, darling, it's not fair on him."

"It's not fair on Joey," wept Cupcake.

Everyone was in tears by now. Even Mrs Costello. Even me. Then Joey went and *really* cracked us up.

"That why I can't have an operation?" he said. "Cos we can't afford it?"

"Oh, sweetheart, no!" His mum sounded horrified. "That's not the reason! If an operation would make you well we'd find the money from somewhere. Even if it was three thousand pounds, we'd find it!"

"Then why not for Cookie?"

"Because you're my very own special little boy!" She tried to hug him, but he pushed her off, sobbing.

"Cookie *my* very own special little boy!"

Joey was hanging on to Cookie like he thought someone might tear him away at any moment.

"Not letting him go, not letting him go!"

"Well…" His mum pulled out a tissue and blotted at her nose with it. "I suppose we don't have to decide immediately."

"No, cos something might turn up," I said. "We might win the lottery!" I was only trying to be positive; there wasn't any need for Cupcake to snap at me and say they didn't do the lottery.

"How can we win if we don't do it?"

"We do it," I said. "My mum does it every week. Maybe she'll win!"

I mean, it's always possible, right? Otherwise, what would be the point? I said this to Cupcake afterwards. She said, "It's like believing in miracles."

I told her that I did believe in miracles. I said, "Somebody's got to win. On the other hand – " cos I do think you have to have a back-up plan – "we can't just sit around waiting. We need the money *now*. There's got to be some way we can get some!"

"Yes, but how?" wailed Cupcake.

"I don't know! Give me time; I'll find a way," I said. "Don't worry!"

I asked Mum, when I got home, whether she knew a way of making money. She said, "If I did, do you really think I'd still be here?"

I said, "Why? Where would you be?"

"The Bahamas, probably. Look, could you just run upstairs for me and give this parcel to Mrs Mackie?

Tell her I took it in for her. OK?"

I said, "Yes, but why the Bahamas?"

"Because it's sunny."

"What about me and Dad and Rosie? Where'd we be?"

"Oh, you'd be there as well, talking nineteen to the dozen, as usual! Just go and take that parcel for me, there's a good girl. And don't be all day because tea's ready."

I said, "How could I be all day, just going up to the next floor?"

"You could," said Mum. "When that mouth of yours gets going, you could be there half the night!"

I don't know why everybody thinks I talk a lot. I only talk when there's stuff to talk about.

I whizzed upstairs with the parcel and hammered at the door of no.12, yelling, "Mrs Mackie, it's Danielle from downstairs!" This was just so's she'd know I wasn't someone wanting to bash her over the head and burgle her. We have quite a lot of burglars living round our way. One of them is Mrs Mackie's son, Shane, except he'd been put away, or so I thought. I was quite surprised when he opened the door. "Hello, Motormouth! What d'you want?"

I said, "I've got a parcel for your mum. And who are you calling Motormouth?"

He said, "You! And don't be cheeky."

He really fancies himself, does Shane. Thinks he's so tough. I'm not scared of him!

I said, "Thought you were away somewhere."

"Yeah? Well, now I'm back, so you just better watch it. Have a bit of respect for your elders and betters."

I said, "You're not that old, and you certainly aren't better!" And then I shot back down the stairs, double quick.

Shane leant over and bawled after me. "Know what? That tongue of yours is gonna get you into trouble one of these days! I'd button it, if I was you."

Someone else going on about me. All I was doing was just passing the time of day!

Dad was coming up the stairs as I reached our landing. He said, "What was all that about?"

"Shane Mackie giving me hassle," I said.

"Which of course you did nothing to provoke?"

I said, "He was the one that started it! He called me Motormouth."

Dad laughed. "I wonder why?"

I said, "*I* don't know. I don't talk any more than anyone else."

"No? Try proving it," said Dad. "See how long you can go without actually saying anything... five minutes is my bet!"

That was when it came to me: my scheme for making money...

CHAPTER FIVE

There are several ways of making money. These are
some of the ones I thought of. You could:

Get a job

Win the lottery

Sell something

Go begging

Rob a bank

Ask people to sponsor us

Well, me and Cupcake obviously couldn't get a job, we were too young. And we couldn't win the lottery cos we didn't do it, and even if we did it could be years before we picked the right numbers. *If ever.* We didn't have anything worth selling, and our mums would be, like, demented if they heard we'd gone begging, so that really only left two possibilities: we could either rob a bank, or we could ask people to sponsor us.

The problem with robbing a bank – apart, of course, from the fact that it would be a VERY BAD thing to do – was that we had no experience and we'd probably go and get caught, like Butch Cassidy and the Sundance Kid. And they'd had *loads* of experience. I was desperate to get the money for poor little Cookie, but I wasn't quite ready to start a life of crime. There was only one thing for it – we would have to throw ourselves on people's mercy and *ask* them for the money.

"You mean, like, begging?" said Cupcake, when I told her about it the next day.

I said, "No! Not begging. A sponsored silence." It was such a brilliant idea! I explained to her how it had come to me last night, when Shane had called me Motormouth. "Then Dad said, '*See how long you can go without actually saying anything.*' And that's when I thought of it!"

"But how would it make money?" said Cupcake.

"We'd be sponsored... so much a minute."

Cupcake, as usual, had to go and put a damper on things. "Who's going to give us money just for keeping quiet?"

I said, "Lots of people, I should think." The way they all went on about me and my mouth, they ought to be only too happy to pay me for not talking for a bit. I said this to Cupcake, but she wrinkled her nose and said, "Where'd we do it?"

I told her, at school. "So they can keep an eye on us and know we're not cheating."

"But suppose we're in a lesson and one of the teachers asks us a question? Then what do we do?"

I said, "Make like a goldfish!" and I gobbled silently, munching on my lips.

"What's that supposed to mean?" said Cupcake.

"Means *I can't talk, I've lost my voice.*"

"Both of us?"

I said, "Yeah! Both of us."

"I dunno." Cupcake shook her head. "I can't see anyone's going to pay us just for doing nothing."

"We won't be doing nothing! We'll be keeping *quiet.*"

"It's still doing nothing."

"So what d'you suggest? We've got to get the money from somewhere! What about your dad? You could try asking your dad!"

Cupcake said that wouldn't be any good. "He already complains about having to pay Mum for me and Joey."

"Seriously?" I said. "But he's your *dad.*"

"I know." Cupcake said it sadly. "But he's got another family now."

I couldn't help thinking what a horrible person Cupcake's dad must be. How could you walk out and leave your own kids? Specially when one of them was sick. I couldn't imagine my dad ever doing it. Cupcake had told me once that it wasn't her dad's fault. "He just couldn't cope. It upset him too much." I guess she felt she had to defend him. She probably still loves him, in spite of everything, which is why I always try to be patient with her. I just take a breath and count up to ten. "*One... two...*" And then I gabble the rest as fast as I can, before she has a chance to go glooming on. "If your dad won't help, it'll have to be up to us. We might at least *try* my idea. Not going to kill us, is it?"

"No. You're right." Cupcake nodded. "We'll do it! We'll tell everyone we've taken a vow of silence." She beamed. "No talking for one whole day... that's no big deal!"

Well! Huh. It might not be for some people. Cupcake quite often goes for minutes at a time without speaking. Me, I don't understand the expression "lost for words". I have simply crowds of them just bursting to get out!

But we'd taken our vow, and we'd explained to everyone what we were doing it for. "For Cookie, for his operation. And for Joey, cos he just loves him *so much*." We swore we wouldn't utter a single solitary syllable for the entire day. Not a sound would escape from us. Not even an *um* or an *ah*. Only if one of the teachers happened to ask us something, and then we would answer, cos we'd have to, but apart from that – zilch! I flicked an imaginary zipper across my lips. A girl called Davina Walker, who has a very suspicious mind, wanted to know who was going to monitor us and make sure we kept to the rules.

I said, "Claire and Livy," but Davina immediately objected. She said, "They can't do it! They're your friends."

Claire bristled at that. She said, "*So what?*" Then Livy weighed in. "Are you saying we can't be trusted?" They almost came to blows before we even began! Some of the boys got excited and thought there was going to be a fight, but Emily Parks told everyone to cool it.

"This is important! We're trying to help Lisa's little brother."

After much heated discussion, it was agreed that Davina would monitor us, along with Emily. Emily is the sort of person who everyone looks up to as she is not only mega brilliant but also very practical. She will end up as a prefect, for sure, if not Head Girl. Me and Cupcake didn't mind Emily sticking with us all day. We could have done without Davina, who is just a busybody at the best of times, but as Cupcake reminded me, "It's all in a good cause."

We'd been going to pin a sheet of paper on the notice board in our classroom so that people could sign their names and say how much they were sponsoring us for, but at the last minute we'd decided against it. We thought one of the teachers might see it and say, "What's all this about?" Schools are so full of rules and regulations; there was almost bound to be one saying you couldn't collect money, even for a good cause, without asking for permission. Cupcake wondered whether we should try asking, but I was worried in case they said no, and then our whole plan would be ruined. So we agreed: teachers must be kept out! We explained this to everyone in our class.

"You can all decide how much you want to sponsor us for, and we'll trust you to be honest about it."

Davina objected that that was not how it was supposed to be done, but nobody took any notice of her. Emily said, "Everybody who wants to support Dani and Lisa, write down in their rough books how much they're going to give."

"It can be as little as you like," said Cupcake.

"Or as much," I said. I didn't want people to be stingy.

"Just imagine," I said to Cupcake, "if the whole of

our year group were to sponsor us!" It could easily happen. Lots of people in our class had said they'd got friends in other classes and would tell them what we were up to. After all, everyone knew Joey and Cookie. "That'd be ninety people," I said. "All giving us money! And if we manage to do the whole day, that's – " I counted on my fingers – "that's seven hours, which means if everyone gave us a pound an hour, that'd be…"

Well, I didn't know what it would be as I'm not very good at mental arithmetic, but quite a lot, obviously. Cupcake worked it out on her calculator. She gasped. "£630!"

I said, "Wow."

We looked at each other.

"Course, I don't expect everyone will sponsor us," said Cupcake.

"No, and they won't all give us a pound an hour," I agreed. "Still, it looks like we'll easily raise enough money!"

It is really, really, really, hard to go for seven whole hours without speaking. Usually in class I keep my fingers crossed that the teachers won't ask me anything, in fact my heart just, like, *plummets* when they say, "Danielle? Perhaps you could give us the answer?" Cos I almost never can. Games are my thing! Not lessons. Now, when I actually prayed for someone to ask me something, just so that I could do a bit of talking, they all ignored me. Cupcake, too. Halfway through the morning she slipped me a note: I FEEL LIKE SCREAMING. If Cupcake felt like screaming, you can imagine how I felt! I wrote a note back, saying, THINK ABOUT JOEY AND COOKIE.

It was the only way I could stop myself from going mad and screeching. I kept repeating it, over and over. *Joey 'n' Cookie. Cookie 'n' Joey.* I even mouthed it at Cupcake, who nodded, and started mouthing it herself. Davina prodded me in the back and hissed, "You were talking!" I mouthed, "Was not." At break she told Emily that I'd been "Talking silently", with my lips. I almost yelled at her, "Lips don't count!" Fortunately Emily got in first and said that "lip moving" was OK so long as no sound came out. I mouthed, "See?"

"Well, you'd just better watch it," said Davina, "cos I've got my eye on you."

She had, too. That girl followed us *everywhere*. She even tried to cram into the loo with me! Then when we went back into the playground she started taunting me about this Year 8 boy who I sort of fancied. I don't even know how she knew that I fancied him, but she's one of those people who's always sticking her sharp, pointy nose in where it doesn't belong. Like I said, a busybody.

"Ooh, look!" she squealed. "There he is! Shall we call him over? Hey! Scotty! Scott Silverman! Someone wants to talk to you!"

God, I nearly *died*. It was just so embarrassing! Especially when he actually came over and asked what the problem was.

Davina said, "No problem! Danielle just wanted to

talk to you. Go on!" She prodded me. "Say something!"

Cupcake clapped a hand to her mouth. I felt my cheeks go sizzling into the red zone.

"Aah, she's shy!" crowed Davina.

"What's going on?" said Scott.

It was Emily who explained that I couldn't speak. "They're on a sponsored silence to help Lisa's little brother keep his dog. He needs an operation and they're trying to raise money."

Scott said, "Oh! OK. I'll give you 50p."

I shot this triumphant glance at Davina. Her plan had backfired! Not that it stopped her trying. At lunch time me and Cupcake had to point to the dishes we wanted, and just beam and nod, or shake our heads. One of the serving ladies got a bit cross and snapped, "A please or a thank you wouldn't go amiss!"

Davina immediately prodded me, going, "You might show some manners!"

Then in afternoon break Mrs Todd, who's like this bug-eyed alien from outer space, absolutely *no* connection with the human race, bawled at me as we rushed past her: "Danielle Cassidy, do that shoe lace up before you trip over and break your neck, and why are you wearing trainers, anyway?"

Oops! I was wearing trainers cos my school shoes had come apart and I didn't have any spare ones. But how was I supposed to tell her??? I sent this agonised gaze in Emily's direction. Yet again, she saved the day. She said, "Oh, Mrs Todd, Dani's lost her voice, she can't even croak."

"Really?" The alien bug eyes raked me up and down. "It still doesn't explain why she's wearing trainers. Don't let me see you in them again!"

And *that* was when I nearly went and blew it. I just felt so grateful to Emily! I opened my mouth to thank her — and just in time Cupcake screamed out, really loud, and drowned the sound of my voice. Needless to say, Davina got all triumphant and gloaty, and danced up and down waving her fingers in my face. "She spoke! She spoke!"

"She *squealed*," said Emily.

"One of them squealed and one of them screamed!" Emily said squealing and screaming was not the same as speaking; it was just making noises.

"But they took a vow of silence!"

"Doesn't include noises," said Emily. "It just means not talking."

"They said not an *um* or an *ah*!"

"They didn't say not a squeal or a screech."

We had actually promised that not a sound would escape us, but as Emily pointed out, you can't breathe without sounds escaping. "Can't expect them to stop *breathing*."

Phew! You could tell Davina wasn't pleased. She'd really wanted to catch me out, she was that sort of person, but nobody, not even Davina, argued with Emily. Emily was far too clever. I said later to Cupcake, though, that it had been a bad moment.

"Cos I *did* speak. I got as far as *Th*— and then you screeched and covered it up. That was quick thinking, that was!"

Cupcake glowed. I suppose I'm usually more likely to be nagging at her to get a move on or make up her mind than congratulate her for speedy thinking. I said, "You don't suppose it counts as cheating, do you?"

"Probably," said Cupcake, "but I don't care! I don't care about anything so long as Cookie can have his operation and get better."

I said, "Tomorrow everyone'll give us their money and then we can tell your mum to go ahead."

"Yes, cos we should have *oodles*," said Cupcake.

We'd asked everyone to pay us at the end of school. I said, "We'll wait at the gates with carrier bags!"

We had one big Sainsbury's bag and one from Tesco's, and as people came by we held them out for them to put their money in. Cupcake's mum, who hadn't known what we were up to, got a bit fussed. She kept saying, "I'm not sure this is right! I'm not sure you ought to be doing this."

Cupcake said, "Mum, we're not forcing anyone."

"No, it's absolutely voluntary," I said.

It didn't stop her fussing. She said it was "Still asking people for money." Well, of course it was! That was the whole point. There's nothing actually *illegal* about asking people to give money to a good cause; not as far as I know. It's not like we were pointing a gun at them, or anything. I think Cupcake's mum is quite an anxious sort of person, and that's where Cupcake gets it from. Fortunately, lots of people dragged their mums over to us and asked them to make a donation, and after that Mrs Costello got a bit happier and decided maybe it was all right.

"Now all we've got to do is count it," gloated Cupcake, as we staggered home with Joey nursing not only Cookie but two big bulging bags of coins on his lap.

We emptied the bags on to the kitchen table and got to work, me and Cupcake and Joey. Joey collected up the notes and the pound coins, cos there weren't so many of them; me and Cupcake did the rest, piling coins into little columns at one end of the table.

Cupcake said she had never seen so much money.

"Cookie money," said Joey.

"There must be hundreds!" Exultantly, I completed yet another column of 2p pieces. They marched up and down the table in rows. Stack after stack of them.

"Got to be *more* than enough," said Cupcake.

But there wasn't! When we added up all the notes, and all the little piles, it only came to £73. It wasn't anywhere near enough! We needed four times that amount.

I cried, "Those mean, skinflinty people!" Most of them had obviously only given us about 5p an hour. Quite a lot of them hadn't given us anything at all. "You'd think they could do better than that!"

"One or two said they'd pay us tomorrow," offered Cupcake.

"One or two's not going to do any good!"

"Oh, girls. After all your hard work." Cupcake's mum sadly shook her head. "You did what you could. You really tried! I think we'll just have to give the money back, and—"

"No!" Joey shrieked, and flung his arms across the table, toppling several piles of coins. "Cookie money! I'm not giving it back!"

"We can raise more," said Cupcake. "We can!" She glared at me, like defying me to contradict her. "We'll think of something else. We'll get the rest of it!"

I didn't say anything; nor did Cupcake's mum. I was just, like, totally deflated. I had been so sure our plan would work! I'd struggled so hard, all day yesterday, not to say so much as a single solitary word, and we hadn't even managed to raise *half* the money we needed. I felt so bad! We'd told Cupcake's mum we'd get the money. We'd promised we'd get it, and now we hadn't, and how was she going to tell Joey that he would have to be parted from his beloved Cookie? Already he was sobbing as he tried to round up all the tumbled piles of coins.

"Cookie money! Cookie money!"

Cupcake said, "Yes, it is. It's Cookie's money, and we're going to get more of it!"

"Maybe… " Her mum gazed despairingly round the kitchen. "Maybe we could have a garage sale, or… "

Her voice trailed off. Even I could see that there wasn't anything that could be sold at a garage sale. Not in the kitchen, not anywhere in the whole house. Some rooms were almost bare. Cupcake, for instance, didn't even have a proper wardrobe, just a rail behind a curtain. My mum and dad are not what you would call well-off, they are always worrying about how to pay the bills, but at least we get to go on holiday every year and have days out now and then. Cupcake doesn't. So I think her mum must be really, really poor. This just made it worse that we couldn't even raise enough money for one poor little dog to have his operation!

Mum asked me, when I got home, why I was looking so glum. "Sky fallen in?"

I said, "No, but sometimes life is just so depressing."

When I told her why, she said that in some ways it was a pity we had ever discovered Cookie. She said that now Joey had bonded with him, it was going to mean heartbreak when they had to be parted.

"It's so not fair!" I wailed.

Mum agreed. She said, "I'm afraid life isn't. That's a lesson we all have to learn."

I said, "I don't mind learning it, but why should Joey have to? He has so much to put up with, and he never complains, and all he wants is his little dog! Cupcake says we'll get the money somehow. She says we'll think of something. But I don't know what we can do!"

"You could always find a treasure map," said Rosie.

I hadn't realised she was there. I turned on her, "Don't be so stupid!"

"I'm not being stupid, it's what people do. They find treasure maps and go and dig up the treasure."

"In your dreams!" I said.

"In *books*," said Rosie.

I made an impatient scoffing sound.

"Dani, she's only trying to help," said Mum.

She wasn't trying to help; she was being *stupid*. I went off in a huff and when she knocked at my bedroom door a few minutes later and demanded to be let in I nearly told her to get lost, except if I had she'd only have gone running to Mum. I opened the door a crack and glowered at her. "What do you want?"

"I want to give you something."

"What?"

She stuck her hand through the door. "For Cookie."

"What is it?"

"For Cookie!" She pushed a bit of crumpled paper at me. I stared, disbelievingly. It was a five-pound note! My annoying little spoilt brat of a sister had given me a *five-pound note*.

"I was saving it up," she said, "but you can have it." I couldn't believe it. I asked Mum, later, if it was OK for me to keep it.

"Of course it is," said Mum. "I didn't put her up to it; it was entirely her own idea. And while we're at it, here's a little something from me as well."

A whole tenner! I cried, "Oh, Mum, thank you,

thank you, thank you!" and flung my arms round her.

"That's all right," said Mum. "It's the least I can do. I just hope you manage to raise the rest of the money."

I told Mum that we had to; I was already ashamed of being so negative. I actually rang Cupcake and apologised. "You're right," I said, "we'll get the money somehow. Even if it means robbing a bank!"

Of course, we didn't rob a bank; but we were about to embark on our life of crime...

CHAPTER SIX

Miracles do happen! I'd said so to Cupcake, and she hadn't believed me. But they do — and one did! It happened to me and Cupcake the very next day, in Cupcake's back garden. Not that we immediately recognised it as a miracle. It wasn't like we suddenly discovered a load of buried treasure or a wad of banknotes tossed over the fence. I don't think miracles are ever that simple. I think what they do is, they point the way, like a sort of signpost: **FOLLOW THIS PATH.** And then it's up to you whether you follow it or not. Sometimes, probably, with a lot of people, they don't even notice. It just goes to show, you have to be on the lookout.

What happened with me and Cupcake, we were in the garden playing with Cookie and racking our brains how to make more money. Cupcake had a pen and a notepad and was writing a list. So far the list had three things on it:

Sponsored run

Sponsored sing

Sponsored sit

The run was my idea; the singing was Cupcake's. But since I can't sing and Cupcake's no use at running, we reckoned we might as well cross them off before we even started. So then we thought maybe we could spend the whole of lunch break sitting absolutely still, like statues, and people could come and watch us and pay us money for every minute we didn't twitch.

I said, "That way, the whole school could give us money... we could make hundreds!"

"Like last time," said Cupcake. "We were going to make hundreds last time."

"Yes, but that was just our year group. This would be the whole school!"

Cupcake said, "Mm... maybe."

I knew I hadn't convinced her. I wasn't really convinced myself. I sighed, and tossed Cookie's ball for him. He scampered after it, on three legs, then suddenly stopped. His tail went down, his head went down. His sides started heaving. Cupcake went into instant panic.

"What's happening? What's happening? What's wrong with him?"

It's just as well that I know about dogs. "It's all right," I said. "He's only being sick."

"But why? What's wrong?"

"He probably didn't chew his food properly. It's what happens with my gran's dog. If she doesn't cut his dinner up small enough, he gollops it all down, then brings it straight back up."

"But he hasn't had any dinner! He had his dinner last night. Oh, God, suppose he's been poisoned?"

Already Cupcake was on her hands and knees, peering at whatever it was that Cookie had sicked up. Cookie peered, too. His tail wagged hopefully.

"What is it?" I said. Something repulsive, I bet.

"Don't know." Cupcake broke a twig off a nearby bush and began poking. "Hey, come and have a look!"

"Do I have to?"

"Yes! There's something here."

A pile of dog sick. I crawled across the grass.

"It's a ring!" said Cupcake.

"Wow!" I suddenly got excited. I snatched at the twig. "Let's have a proper look... this could be valuable!"

"*Ugh.*" Cupcake shied away. "It's all black and gungy!"

"Only cos it's been inside him. It's stomach acid."

"It's disgusting!"

"You were the one prodding at it. Let's take it back to my place and get it cleaned up!"

Cupcake said, "My mum's got cleaning stuff."

"Yeah, but she'd want to know what we wanted it for. We can be on our own if we go back to my place. My mum's out shopping." Mum was out shopping, Dad was at work. In other words, *nobody around to ask questions*. I just felt, instinctively, that it would be better if our mums didn't know. The start of the slippery slope…

"First thing to do," I said, "is soak it in vinegar."

"What for?" said Cupcake.

"It's what you do." It was what my dad had done when he'd dug up an ancient spoon in my gran's back garden. Not my doggy gran; the other one. The spoon had been black, just like the ring. Dad had been really excited! He'd soaked it in vinegar and cleaned it with special polish, then looked at it through a magnifying glass to see if it was silver.

"How can you tell?" said Cupcake.

I said, "I'm not sure… they have these little marks." *Hall*marks; that's what Dad had called them. "He looked them up on the computer. If it's got the right sort of marks it means it's real silver."

Gran's spoon had had the right marks. Dad had wanted to sell it, but Gran had said no, she fancied the idea of having a real silver spoon.

"But she *could* have sold it," I said. "People give you money for real silver."

Me and Cupcake looked at each other.

"How much?" said Cupcake.

"Dunno, but I think you'd get more for jewellery than for a spoon," I said.

We couldn't wait for that ring to be cleaned up! As soon as we'd soaked it and polished it, so that it was all bright and shiny, I held it at an angle and squinted at it.

"Is there a mark? Is there a mark?" Cupcake was almost jumping up and down with impatience.

"There's a… a thing that looks like an anchor, and a… a lion."

"What does that mean? Does that mean it's real silver?"

"Not sure till we've looked it up. But look! Blue stones." There was a whole little cluster of them, arranged in the shape of a flower. "They could be sapphires!"

Cupcake's eyes went very big and round. "*Sapphires*," she breathed. "They're precious!"

"Let's go and look up the marks!"

We raced to the computer and clicked on to Google. I said, "What shall I put in? Silver, or hallmarks?"

"Both," said Cupcake. "What sort of marks did your gran's spoon have?"

"Can't remember… there are loads of them. All different. They tell you where things were made. Look, look!" I pointed jubilantly. "There it is!"

An anchor, and a lion, just like on our ring. We

peered closer at the screen.

"Made in Birmingham," said Cupcake. "Is that OK?"

"Course it is! Doesn't matter where it's made, just so long as it's real silver. It could be worth a fortune!" I turned and scooped up Cookie, who was busy trying to dig a hole in the carpet. "He's our little fortune cookie!"

It was a solemn moment. "You honestly think we could get something for it?" said Cupcake.

"Why not? It's *silver*."

"But what if someone asks where it's come from?"

"It came out of our dog. That's why he's our fortune cookie!"

"Yes, but... before that. Before he swallowed it."

"Could have come from anywhere. It's not our problem, is it?"

Cupcake said, "N-no... I s'ppose not."

"Well, it's not! We can't help what he did before we got him. He could have done all sorts of things! You can't blame us."

"No. In any case," said Cupcake, sounding a bit bolder, "we don't actually *know*. Not for certain."

I could guess what she was thinking, cos I was thinking it, too. We were both remembering the day we had seen Cookie in the old lady's garden, tossing something bright and shiny into the air, and the old woman had come running out and shouted and taken it away from him. And then we'd seen him doing it again, a few days later; only this time the old woman hadn't come out...

"Still not our problem," I said. "I'll tell you what our problem is."

"What?"

"Where are we going to sell it?" It was a *big* problem. "If we go into a jeweller's," I said, "they'll only cheat us."

"Either that, or ask questions."

I agreed that questions were the last thing we wanted. It is very difficult, sometimes, being eleven years old. Well, I'm twelve, now, and I can't really say it's got any easier. There are just so many things you can't do! Like selling a valuable ring that has been sicked up by *your own puppy* without a) being ripped off, just because you're kids, or b) reported to the police.

"Cos that's what they'd do," said Cup. "They'd think we'd stolen it."

"Well, we haven't," I said fiercely. "It belongs to us and there's got to be some way we can get the money for it!"

"We could try putting a card in a shop window," said Cupcake. "Mum found Joey's tricycle from a shop window."

"Mm… " I wasn't sure I liked the sound of that. "We'd have to give a telephone number. Anyone could just ring up! You could get nutters and all sorts."

My dad's always going on eBay. He's really into finding bargains! And selling things. But I knew they wouldn't let me and Cupcake on there. *Too young.* Like you can't act responsibly, just because you're eleven years old.

"There's got to be something!" said Cupcake.

Neither of us suggested going to my mum and dad, or Cupcake's mum. We both knew what *they'd* do.

"*Go to the police.*" We chanted it, together. "Of course – " Cupcake said a bit uncertainly – "there might be a reward."

I said, "Yes, and there might not. We can't afford to take the chance!"

"It's not really breaking the law," said Cupcake, "is it?"

I told her very firmly that it wasn't. "It's *our* ring that came out of *our* dog and we're going to get the money for it!"

We decided what we would do: we would go to the shopping centre and look in all the jewellers' windows and check out the prices.

"That way," I said, "we'll know a bit better what it's worth."

In the meantime, we had to find somewhere safe to put it. It is amazing how difficult it is to find safe places

– that is, places your mum won't go stumbling into while she's dusting, or vacuuming, or putting stuff away. I thought maybe it would be best if I wore it round my neck on a piece of string, but Cupcake screamed out in horror.

"You might get mugged!"

I said, "Nobody would know it was there."

"But they might mug you anyway, and then they'd find it. Or what if the string went and broke?"

I said, "String doesn't break," but she insisted that we had to find some safe place. "Somewhere in your bedroom."

"Like where?" I said. "For instance?"

We both stared round. Cupcake said, "Maybe we could hide it in a drawer… like under a pile of clothes, or something." But that wasn't any good. Who knew when Mum might have one of her mad fits and start rearranging things, or "weeding out", like the time she took my favourite T-shirt to use as a floor cloth?

"But, Dani," she said, when I protested, "it was a *rag*!"

It might have been a rag, but it was *my* rag. And I loved it! I was relating the tale with much bitterness to Cupcake when we heard the front door open and Dad's voice ring out: "Anyone at home?"

Cupcake squeaked, "Your dad! Do something!"

I didn't hesitate. Quick as a flash, I yanked off one of my trainers, stuffed the ring into my sock, down over the toes, and shoved my foot back in. Cupcake watched, open-mouthed. Astonished, I expect, by the speed of my reaction. I think I am quite good in emergencies! I am not one of those people that go all to pieces.

We went out into the hall. I said, "Hi, Dad!" Cupcake, who is always very polite, said, "Hello, Mr Cassidy."

Dad sprang round, in mock terror. "Don't shoot, I give in!" He put his hands in the air. "Take my money but spare my life!" And then he laughed and said, "How ya doin', Cupcake? Surprised the police haven't caught up with you two yet!"

It is Dad's idea of a joke; he is always teasing us about being outlaws, like Butch Cassidy and the Sundance Kid. Usually we joke back, but this time Cupcake went bright red, like we really *were* wanted by the police. I knew I had to rescue the situation. Cupcake was practically bursting into flames.

"We're just taking Cookie back home," I said, "then we're off into town to do a couple of bank jobs."

"And the best of luck!" said Dad.

"He thinks it's funny," whispered Cupcake, as we left the flat.

"Well, it is," I said. "Imagine us marching into a bank!"

"He wouldn't think it was so funny if he knew what you'd got in your sock," said Cupcake. "And *suppose you get mugged?*"

I said, "What if I do? Who's going to look in my sock?"

"In the hospital, they would. If you had to go there after being mugged!"

It's no use arguing with her. Once Cupcake gets an idea into her head, there's no shifting it. All the way up the road, she was seeing muggers wherever she looked. Black muggers, white muggers. Men, women and children muggers. Even, once, a little old lady mugger. She said, "You read about these things. Some old ladies can be really violent!"

Not any of the ones we met, though an old lady on the bus, as we went into town, did ask me if I needed to sit down. She thought I'd twisted my ankle! I said, "Thank you, but it's all right, I just have a bunion." I'm not quite sure what a bunion is, exactly, except that you get them on your feet and they're painful. One of my grans is always going on about her bunions. In fact what had happened was that the ring had somehow managed to get itself wedged between two of my toes and was rubbing them raw. I told Cupcake that I was in agony, but she wasn't the least bit sympathetic. She just said that it was "A stupid place to put it." Just for that, when we got off the bus I made her stand guard while

I took my trainer off and stuck my fingers down my sock, trying to wriggle the ring free of my toes. That really gave her the jitters!

There are loads of jewellery shops in the town centre. There're posh ones, and tatty ones, and all sorts in between. We didn't bother with the tatty ones, cos they only did cheap stuff. Our ring was *quality*. It was so quality we couldn't find anything to compare it to!

"Maybe being silver it isn't worth anything," moaned Cupcake.

I said, "Course it is!" But even I was starting to get a bit worried. All the really expensive rings seemed to be made of gold. "I think gold's really vulgar," I said. "Ours is loads prettier!"

"Not much good if it's not worth anything," said Cupcake. "For all we know, it could've come out of a Christmas cracker!"

I said, "They don't put real silver rings in crackers. Let's go and ask!"

Cupcake screeched, "Fudge! No!" but once I have come to a decision that's it. There's no stopping me. Boldly I marched through the door of this shop called The Jewel Box and went up to the counter. The girl who was standing behind it gave me this snooty look, like I was some kind of disgusting pimple on the point of bursting. In this really bored tone of voice she drawled, "Can I help you?"

I said, "Yes. I'd like to know how much—" And then I remembered: the ring was still in my sock. Oops! "'Scuse me," I said, "I have a stone in my shoe." Well, it was true, I did have! I had a whole cluster of them. Beautiful blue sapphires that had to be worth a *fortune*. I bent down and thrust my fingers into my sock, with Cupcake hovering nervously at my side. "I'd like to know how much this ring is worth," I said. "Please!"

You could tell she didn't really want to be bothered, but she took the ring off me and told us to wait and she'd get someone to look at it. Cupcake was all jitters again. "I bet she's gone to ring the police!"

Defiantly I said, "What if she has? They can't do us for anything. It's our ring; it came out of our dog!" I said this to reassure Cupcake; I wasn't really feeling that confident, especially when the girl came back with an important-looking man in a suit.

"This is a very interesting ring," he said. "May I enquire where you got it from?"

I thought Cupcake was going to pass out on the spot; I could actually *feel* her shaking. Fortunately, my brain had gone whizzing into overdrive.

"It's not mine," I said. "It belongs to my gran. She wants to know how much it's worth, so I said I'd come and ask. She can't get about any more. She's pretty old – she has these bunions. On her feet. They're really painful!"

"I see. Well… it's hard to put a price on it. Has your grandmother had it a long time?"

"I don't know," I said. "She didn't tell me."

"I only ask, because it's obviously quite old. Victorian, I should think."

"It's got to be worth quite a lot, though," I said, "what with the sapphires?"

"Yes, they're not sapphires, they're what's known as aquamarine. Still, very pretty. And probably worth a fair bit."

"What's 'a fair bit'?" I said.

"Well, off the top of my head... "

What was he talking about, off the top of his head? That was just, like, totally *meaningless*.

"My gran was hoping she'd get maybe £200 for it?" I said sternly, to show I didn't think much of this top of the head stuff. "*At least* £200, my gran said."

He agreed that £200 was quite possible.

"Maybe more?" Cupcake kicked me, very hard, on the ankle. I ignored her. I knew she wanted me to shut up, and take the ring back, and get out, but we needed to know! "Maybe... *£300? £500? £1000?*"

"I wouldn't go as high as £1000," he said.

"But it's silver!"

"It is indeed, and a fine piece of craftsmanship. It

might well fetch somewhere in the region of £300. I suggest you leave it with me, and I'll get it properly valued. How about that?"

I heard a quick intake of breath from Cupcake. "I can't leave it," I said. "My gran wants it back."

"She shall have it back! Let me give you a receipt."

I shook my head. It was all I could do to stop myself snatching the ring and bolting from the shop. I was beginning to feel I might have made a bit of a mistake. "I daren't go back without it," I said. "My gran'll go ballistic!"

"Well, then, give me your gran's telephone number, and I'll ring her when I've got a valuation."

I said, "How can you get a valuation if you haven't got the ring?"

"I've got it up here." He tapped the side of his head. "I'll do some ferreting about and let her know. What's her number?"

I am so bad at numbers! My mind instantly froze. It was Cupcake who blurted out what sounded to me like a real, genuine telephone number. I hoped it wasn't! The next thing he wanted was my gran's name. But I am OK at names. I said, "Mrs Green!" And then I took back the ring and forced myself to walk very slowly and calmly out of the shop. Cupcake nearly went and ruined it by scuttling ahead of me like a frightened mouse, but I couldn't really say anything considering she was the one who had to come to my rescue with the telephone number.

"Was it a real one?" I said.

Cupcake said no, she'd made it up. "What about Mrs Green?"

Proudly, I said that I'd made that up, too. "It's what's known as thinking on your feet."

"D'you think we ought to do some more thinking on our feet and get out of here?" said Cupcake.

I said yes, I did. "I bet he's trying to call that number right now!"

We didn't relax until we were on the bus on the way home. The ring was back in my sock, and we were gloating.

"Three hundred pounds! That'd be more than enough."

"Except we still don't know how we're going to sell it," said Cupcake.

"No," I said, "that's true."

It was a real problem. We were still discussing it as we got off the bus and turned up Gliddon Road towards the Estate. Shane Mackie was hanging about at the entrance. He does a lot of hanging about. Usually, I take no notice of him; today, for some reason, I found myself saying "Hi".

Shane said, "What d'you want, Motormouth?"

"What's it to you?" I said.

"What you bin up to?"

I said, "We haven't been up to anything."

"Don't come that with me," said Shane. "You got guilt written all over you!" And then, as we walked on past him, he called after us. "You bin nickin' stuff?"

I turned, and stuck up a finger. "Honestly!" I said, "Just cos *he's* been done for—" And then I stopped. It had suddenly come to me: the solution to our problem!

"What, what?" demanded Cupcake.

I said, "Shane Mackie... maybe he could sell it for us!"

CHAPTER SEVEN

"But he's a criminal!" said Cupcake.

I explained that that was the very reason he could be useful to us. "We could sell the ring to him, and he could sell it to... someone else! He knows people."

"*Criminal* people," said Cupcake.

"Not necessarily," I said.

Cupcake looked at me, like, *You don't really believe that.*

"Well, all right," I said, "maybe some of them might be. So what? So long as he gives us the money... it's nothing to do with us what he does with the ring. *Is it?*"

"Suppose not," said Cupcake.

"Well, it's not! I vote we go and talk to him."

"What, now?"

"Why not? Hey, Shane!" I turned, and waved at him. He stayed where he was, slouched against the wall.

"What d'you want?"

"I wanna talk to you!"

"So talk."

He obviously wasn't going to move. I'd have rather he'd come to us, cos where he was it was like this really narrow alleyway between two buildings. Still, if you're dealing with criminals I guess you have to be prepared to lurk about in dark places. And, anyway, it was only Shane. I set off towards him, with Cupcake creeping after me. Shane said, "What d'you wanna talk about?"

"This." I fished the ring from out my sock and held it up for him to see, not getting too near in case he tried to grab it and run. "Thought we might do some business."

"Business with you? You've gotta be joking!"

"I'm not joking," I said. "I'm dead serious."

"Yeah? Well, sorry. Not interested."

"You haven't even looked!" I took a step closer, Cupcake hovering and quivering at my side. Daringly, I stretched out my hand, palm upwards, ready to snatch it back if he made a move. "See?"

He dismissed it with a curl of the lip. "Junk!"

I said, "That shows how much you know. It's not junk, it's an antique. Solid silver."

"So what you showing me for?"

"Thought you might like to sell it for us."

"And why'd I wanna do that?"

"I dunno! Make some money?"

A gleam came into his eye. I could see that he was tempted. "You mean, like, take a cut?"

I said, "Something like that."

"It'd have to be at least fifty per cent if I'm running all the risks."

"There aren't any risks," I said.

"So why not sell it yourself?"

I said, "Cos I'm only eleven, and they'd cheat me."

"What makes you think I wouldn't?"

"I expect you would," I said, "if I let you."

"Yeah? And how'd you propose stopping me?"

"Just cos I'm eleven," I said, "doesn't mean I'm stupid! I'd want the money up front." I thought that was a good expression, *up front*. I'd heard my dad use it. It made it sound like I meant business. Which I did!

Shane said, "Up front? Who are you kidding?"

I told him that I wasn't kidding anyone. "This ring's worth at least £300. All we want is £225!"

His eyes had gone all shifty. He said, "Let's have a proper look."

Cupcake gave a little squeak.

"It's genuine," I said. "It's got hallmarks. And we've had it valued!"

He sneered. "You think I was born yesterday? I don't part with the cash till I've examined the goods!"

Just for a minute I couldn't think what to do; I felt sure if I handed him the ring, he'd take off. Then I had an idea: if he took off with the ring, he'd have to take off with me, as well!

"Hold this," I said to Cupcake. I gave her the ring, removed both the laces from my trainers, knotted them together, threaded one end through the ring, tying it really tight, and told Cupcake to tie the other end round my wrist. "All right," I said, "now you can look at it – out here, not in the alleyway!"

He laughed, like he was really amused, but he peeled himself away from the wall and came out into the open.

"See?" I said. "Hallmarks! And those blue stones, they're... aqua something."

"Marine," said Cupcake.

"Aquamarine. Very valuable!"

Shane said a rude word beginning with B, which I've noticed that boys use quite a lot. I once tried saying it at home only Mum told me to go and wash my mouth out.

"Valuable, my *****!" The little stars are because he said another rude word. "Pretty, though. It might be worth something."

"I told you," I said. "It's worth £300!"

"So where'd you get it from?"

I said, "None of your business!"

"It is if you nicked it."

"We didn't nick it!" I said scornfully. "We're not thieves!"

"It's *ours*," said Cupcake. "It *belongs* to us."

"Expect me to believe that?"

"If you must know," I said, "Cupcake's gran left it to her when she died. Didn't she?" Cupcake looked frightened, but nodded. "Now she wants to sell it cos we need the money."

Shane said, "Why? What d'you need it for?"

Like it was anything to do with him!

"It's for my little brother's puppy," said Cupcake. "He's got to have an operation and my mum can't afford it. That's why we need the money."

"Yeah?"

"Yeah!"

Shane looked again at the ring. He flicked his tongue out, over his lips. "Let's have another gander at those hallmark thingies."

"They're genuine!" I said.

"OK," said Shane. "I'll tell you what I'm prepared to do. Against my better judgement, just to help you out... I'll take it off you for a straight £100."

"Hundred's no good," I said. "Hundred and twenty or nothing."

I thought for a minute he was going to say, in that case nothing. But greed got the better of him! I knew it would. He said, "Right, here's the deal. I'll do a bit of asking around. If I like what I hear, I'll get you your money. If not, forget it! Either way, you just better not be having me on! Cos if you are, there'll be repercussions. Know what I mean?"

We nodded solemnly. I wasn't sure what repercussions were, but obviously something undesirable.

"Nobody takes me for a ride and gets away with it. I'll meet you down here at ten o'clock and we'll do the deal."

I said, "We can't meet at ten o'clock, we're not allowed out that late."

"Oh, boo hoo, you poor little things… not allowed out!"

"No, and we're not meeting here, either," I said. "We'll meet on the second floor, by the lifts. At *five*."

"It'll have to be tomorrow, in that case. I need time to get the readies."

I suppose that by readies he meant money. I wondered where he was going to get it from; I just hoped he wasn't going to go and rob someone.

"I'd like to have the ring back now," I said. "Please."

He made this loud scoffing sound as he tossed it to me on the end of the shoelace.

"Think I couldn't have cut and run if I'd wanted?" He shook his head, like he really pitied me for being so dumb. "You've got no idea who you're dealing with!"

It did make me feel a bit apprehensive. I mean, I've known Shane Mackie all my life. My mum knows his mum. He even used to babysit me when I was little. But that was years ago. He'd just been a bit loud in those days; now he was a criminal.

"See you tomorrow," he said. "And don't forget to bring the goods."

I said, "Don't you forget to bring the money!"

Cupcake said afterwards that I shouldn't have cheeked him, but the way I see it, you can't afford to show fear.

"It'll be OK," I told her. "We won't hand over the goods till he's given us the money."

"I wish it was all over!" Cupcake said. "I'm going home, now. I expect I'll have nightmares."

I thought, poor old Cupcake. She really wasn't cut out for life in the fast lane. Me, I was quite enjoying it. I like a bit of a challenge.

In the lift I bumped into a friend of Mum's, a woman called Mrs Harris who lives on the fifth floor. After complaining about the smell of sick – the lifts always smell of sick, and sometimes of other stuff as well – she said, "Tell your mum that I've finally had enough. Give me notice in, didn't I? You tell her! *Straw that broke the camel's back.*"

I found Mum in the kitchen. I said, "Mrs Harris said to tell you that she's had enough and she's given her notice in."

"About time, too!" said Mum. "I've been nagging her for ages. You know who she worked for, don't you? Old Lady Neverpoop who you got the dog from!"

"She's a *lady?*" I said.

"Likes to think so, giving herself airs and graces. Did Trudi say what happened?"

"She just said it was the straw that broke the camel's back."

"I must give her a bell," said Mum. "Find out. Was she on her way in?"

I said, "I s'ppose." I was still gobsmacked at the thought of that horrid old woman being a lady. I'd never met a lady before. Me and Cupcake hadn't half given her some lip! Well, Cupcake mostly. I wondered how she'd feel when I told her. Abusing a *lady*…

As we sat down to tea Mum said, "Well, the worm's turned… Trudi's finally done it. Given her notice in."

Dad said, "Yeah?"

"Last straw, apparently."

"Oh yeah?"

"The old bag accused her of stealing! Can you imagine?"

Dad said, "Yeah?"

I knew when Dad kept saying "Yeah" all up and down the scale like that, he wasn't really listening; he was concentrating more on the telly. *I* was listening! I was all ears.

"Stealing what?" I said.

"Oh, some ring she couldn't find. Probably took it off and can't remember where she put it. She actually threatened Trudi with the police! Well, Trudi wasn't standing for that. No way! She's been cleaning for that woman nearly ten years, and this is all the thanks she gets."

"*Did* she go to the police?" I said.

"I've no idea, I just know Trudi walked out right there and then."

"So was it a very valuable ring?"

"I suppose so; I don't know. That's not the point! The point *is*..."

Mum went rattling on, but now I wasn't listening, either. I was trying to decide whether it made any difference, knowing for sure that *our* ring that *our* dog had sicked up had actually belonged to the old woman. After a lot of mental tussling, I came to the conclusion that it could only be a good thing. If the ring had belonged to anyone else, like, say, someone had lost it in the park, then it would be like finding a bag, or a purse, or a pile of money; you'd have to take it to the police. But Cookie had been *given* to us, and that meant whatever was inside him had been given to us as well. I didn't see any reason why we shouldn't sell the ring to pay for his operation. It was only fair!

I felt a whole lot happier once I'd worked that out. Shane might be a criminal, and the people he knew might be criminals, but me and Cupcake weren't doing anything wrong.

I explained this to Cupcake when we met next day by the lift on the second floor. I'd told her to be early, so I could explain my plan. I'd worked it all out! We were going to get *into* the lift, and press the button for the top floor.

"And that's when we'll do it... on the way up, so's he can't run off without giving us the money."

Clever, or what? I thought it was! I thought it was a really smart move. Cupcake as usual could only see problems. Like, what if someone else was in there?

I said, "We'll just wait till they get out."

"What if they don't get out until we reach the top?"

"Then we press the button for the basement and go all the way down!"

Oh, but what if someone *else* presses the button? What if someone gets in while we're still only halfway there? What if *no one* gets in and he mugs us?

I said, "He's not going to mug us!"

"You don't know that," said Cupcake. And then she opened her mouth and wailed, "I feel like a criminal!"

So that was when I told her: we *weren't* criminals. I gave her the story of the ring. How Mum's friend had been accused of stealing it and had handed in her notice.

"Mum says, not before time. She's a really *horrible* old woman. Fancy accusing someone of stealing, when all the time it's her own dog! Except he's our dog now, and anything that's inside him is ours as well. It's our ring, and we can do what we like with it."

Cupcake said, "Yes, I know! But I get scared."

"You don't want to be scared of Shane Mackie," I

★ 146 ☆

said. "I remember one time he babysat me, I threw up all over him... he didn't half yell!"

I told her to just stare at Shane very hard and imagine him covered in bright yellow sick. Cupcake was grateful for that. She said it made her feel a bit braver.

I might as well admit it made me feel a bit braver, too. I'd thought my idea was so brilliant! It wasn't till we were actually all shut up together, going up to the top floor – very *slowly* – that I began to wonder if I might have made a mistake. I mean, how many times in movies do you see two people getting into a lift and only one getting out?

Quickly, before I could freak myself out, I stared very hard at Shane's right shoulder, picturing all the bright yellow sick. I could feel Cupcake doing the same thing, standing transfixed at my side. Shane said, "What you two looking at?"

"Oh! Nothing," I said. "I thought a bird had splodged on you, but it must just be the light."

"Or maybe it's the pattern," said Cupcake.

"Or the colours."

"Yes! The colours. Sort of…"

"*Green*," I said.

"And brown," said Cupcake.

"And yellowy."

We were burbling rubbish; we couldn't seem to stop. "Look, cut it out!" said Shane. "This is a business deal, not a flaming tea party. You brought that ring?"

I said, "You brought the money?" I was pretty scared, I don't mind admitting it. But I didn't want him to know; I had to stand up to him.

"Keep your wig on," said Shane. "I did a bit of asking around; I got the money. But I don't want your mum coming down on me like a ton of bricks!"

He glared at Cupcake as he said it. Cupcake clutched nervously at my sleeve. I said, "What's her mum got to do with it? It's my friend's ring, it was left to her. She can do whatever she likes with it."

"Yeah? Well, I don't want no questions. OK? Her

mum asks where it's gone, you say you lost it. You don't bring me into it. You got that?"

I said that we had. "What about the money?"

"All in good time," said Shane. "Don't push your luck."

"But w—"

"I said, don't push your luck!" He suddenly plunged his hand into the back pocket of his jeans, causing both of us to spring backwards, in a panic. I distinctly heard Cupcake go, "Eek!" I don't *think* I squealed, though I may have done.

"Here's your poxy money! Where's the ring?"

I felt quite faint with relief. He was actually holding out a wodge of notes! I grabbed them from him and shoved them at Cupcake.

"Count it!" I said.

"Trust me," said Shane, "it's all there. Now, gimme the goods!"

By now, we'd reached the top floor. The doors had opened, and to my huge relief a couple of people were getting in. I bent down to fiddle with my shoe, scooping out the ring and slipping it into Shane's hand as I stood up. He grunted.

"Just remember," he hissed, as we reached his floor, "if you've bin having me on I'll be back!"

I knew he would. But as I said to Cupcake, we hadn't been having him on, so there was nothing to worry about.

"We've got the money and Cookie can have his operation!"

CHAPTER EIGHT

Now that we had the money, I was all for rushing straight back to Cupcake's place to give it to her mum. She would be so relieved! And Joey would be so happy. I couldn't wait to see his face! It was Cupcake who stopped me. She pointed out that if we gave the money to her mum now, on a Sunday evening, her mum would want to know where we'd got it from.

"We could always tell her I got it."

"She'd still want to know where it came from."

"We could say... one of my grans gave it to me?"

"And then what happens next time my mum talks to your mum? They're always talking! She'd say how kind of your gran, and your mum would say what do you mean, and then my mum'd—"

"Yeah, OK!" I waved a hand, suddenly impatient. I knew that she was talking sense. Her mum would be suspicious, the way grown-ups are. And if we told her the truth, that Cookie had sicked up the ring and we'd sold it to our friendly neighbourhood thug, she'd go tearing round to my mum and dad in a fit of panic. Then *my* mum and dad would get in a panic. It would be "*What have you done?*" And "*Dani, how could you?*" Mum would tell me off for even just talking to Shane.

"You know that boy's no good!"

Dad would probably want to go thundering upstairs to threaten him. He's got a temper, my dad. He once told Shane if he didn't stop revving his bike at 11 o'clock at night he'd knock his block off.

I looked at the wodge of notes Cupcake was holding. Rather lamely, I said, "So what d'you think we should do?" It's not very often I'm at a loss for ideas; I'm usually the one coming up with them. I'm usually *buzzing* with them. But now we'd actually got the money it was like my brain had gone and shut down. That's it! Finish!

"*I* think…" Cupcake said slowly, working things out, "I think we should tell Mum we're going to do that thing we were talking about… that sitting still thing? We'll tell her people are going to sponsor us for every minute we manage not to move."

I said, "*Yesss!*"

"But I think," said Cupcake, "that we'd really have to do it, cos otherwise it would be like telling lies. I know we probably wouldn't make any actual money, but that doesn't matter now. We don't *need* to make any money. It's just…"

"We don't want to upset your mum."

"This is it," said Cupcake. "She's got enough to worry about."

"Let's go and tell her!"

Cupcake's mum seemed a bit doubtful when we said we were going to do a sit-in. "You're trying so hard, both of you, but we're still only a quarter of the way there! And your friends have been so good, I'm not sure you should ask them for any more money."

"Mum, it'll be all right!" said Cupcake.

"Honestly," I said, "they *like* supporting good causes."

"But we need over £200! I'm seriously beginning to think – " she dropped her voice to a whisper, even though Joey was in another room – "I'm seriously beginning to think we shall have to call it a day. It's not even as if I could borrow the money – I'd simply never be able to pay it back. And the longer it goes on, the more unfair it is on Joey. And on Cookie! I'm so, so sorry, girls, after all the effort you've put in. It's entirely my fault; I should have stood firm right at the start. It would have been easier for all of us."

"Mrs Costello, *please*," I said. "We're going to get the money, I promise!"

Cupcake's mum shook her head. She said, "Oh, Dani, I don't know. That poor little dog is in pain, and—"

"And Joey loves him!" cried Cupcake. "And he loves Joey! You can't separate them, Mum. You can't!" She marched across the room and flung open the door of the lounge. "Look!" Joey and Cookie were cuddled up together on the sofa, watching television. Well, Joey was watching television. Cookie was curled nose to tail, blissfully quivering in his sleep.

Joey looked across at us and beamed. "Cookie's having dreams!"

I thought for a truly terrible moment that Cupcake's mum was going to burst into tears. I know the signs! I don't cry very much myself, but when I do my lips start kind of rippling and my eyes go all shimmery. I said, "Please, Mrs Costello! We can do it, I know we can!"

"Just one more day," begged Cupcake. "That's all we need."

Cupcake's mum hesitated, then said all right, she would give us till the end of the week. "After that—"

She couldn't bring herself to finish the sentence. She rushed out of the room, and I knew that this time she really was crying. It's very disturbing when grown-ups cry; you don't expect it of them. They are meant to be the ones in control. I find it quite scary.

Joey had seen that his mum was upset, and that made him upset as well. He wanted to know what he had done. We told him that he hadn't done anything, but he grew angry and banged his fist on the arm of the sofa, shouting, "Cos of me! Cos of me!"

"Joey, it isn't!" I said.

He gave me such a look. When I sat down next to him and tried to cuddle him, he flailed with his arms, pushing me away; he struggled to his feet and tried to go after his mum, but his legs wouldn't carry him, which made him scream with frustration and punch out at Cupcake as she went to his aid. She was anxious to assure me afterwards, as we took Cookie for a walk round the block, that "Joey isn't really like that!" As if I didn't know. I told her there was no need to explain, but she obviously wanted to. She said that Joey was getting weaker all the time.

"There's things he used to be able to do just a few months ago that now he can't. He knows it makes Mum unhappy, and he feels it's all his fault!"

"At least we've got the money for Cookie," I said. "That's something!"

Cupcake said it was more than just something. "It's the most important thing we've ever done in our whole life. Cos if Joey didn't have Cookie I think he'd just give up."

It made it all worthwhile. Even if we *had* become criminals.

Next day at school, I was sitting back to back with Cupcake on a fallen tree trunk on the playing field, trying my hardest not to move, not even to *twitch*. I kept repeating to myself: *If Joey didn't have Cookie, he would just give up.* There wasn't really any need for us to keep so still; it wasn't like we were expecting people to give us money. It was more a point of... honour, I suppose. We'd told Cupcake's mum we were doing a sit-in, so that's what we had to do. Claire and the others couldn't understand it.

"Are you playing at statues?" said Claire. "Or are you training to be living sculptures?"

I said, "Something like that."

I did my best to speak without even moving my lips. Livy wanted to know what would happen if she poked us. "Like this!"

I said, "*Don't.*"

"She moved!" said Davina.

"So would you," said Livy, "if I poked you... like this!"

Davina gave a loud shriek.

"Are you trying to raise more money?" said Emily.

"Cos if you are, we want to know the rules."

Cupcake said, "There aren't any rules… we're just *doing* it."

"Could one ask why?" said Emily. That really is the way Emily speaks. She's ever so intellectual. "I don't want to pry, but—"

"It's yoga," said Cupcake.

Oh! That was so inspired. Next thing we know, they're all at it, hurling themselves down on to the grass and bending their bodies into weird shapes.

"You know, you are meant to *move* occasionally," said Lucy. "Not just sit around like blocks of cement."

I swivelled my eyes towards her; she seemed to have tied herself into some sort of complicated knot. I thought it would be fun if she couldn't undo herself and we had to carry her into school with her limbs all tangled up. Claire had one leg hooked behind her neck. Davina was staring into space with this soppy smile on her lips. She looked ridiculous. They all looked ridiculous! I started to giggle, and that made me shake, and that set Cupcake off, so that very soon we were rolling about on the ground and that was the end of our sit-in. We'd lasted less than fifteen minutes.

"But what's important," I said, "is that we *did* it."

Cupcake said, "Yes, and we don't actually have to *say* that's where we got the money from. I know Mum will *think* that it is."

"As long as we don't actually *tell* her."

Cupcake's mum wasn't coming to meet us that day as Joey had an appointment with a specialist up in London, which meant they wouldn't be back till about six o'clock. Me and Cupcake were going to collect Cookie and take him for a walk, then we were all going back to my place for tea.

"We'll be able to tell Mum we've already counted the money and got it changed into notes," said Cupcake happily as we walked round the park.

"Yes, but how?" I said. "How did we do it?" You have to think of these things; you have to have every detail worked out. "It's no good saying we went into a bank cos I bet *they* wouldn't change it for us."

Cupcake said, "But it's our money! That wouldn't be fair!"

I told her that life wasn't, when you were only eleven years old.

"So what are we going to say?"

The answer came to me in a flash. "We'll say we took it into the Office for safekeeping and Mrs Mlada changed it for us."

"Oh, brilliant!" said Cupcake. "You could be a criminal mastermind!"

She may be right – I do seem able to plot and plan, and come up with cunning ideas. But there must be other jobs I am cut out for, apart from a criminal mastermind. Like if I can't be a TV celeb, I wouldn't mind being a detective. That way, with my devious brain, I could get to outwit all the bad guys!

While we were having tea, Mum asked us what was

happening about Cookie. Proudly we told her that we had managed to raise enough money for his operation. She was very surprised! She said, "Well, congratulations! I never would have thought it. You must have worked really hard – and all your friends must have been extremely generous."

"I was generous," said Rosie. "I gave them something."

Mum said, "Yes, you did, and I'm sure Cookie's very grateful."

Rosie beamed. She said, "I *was* saving up to buy myself a present, and now I can't, but I don't mind... I'd rather make someone else happy."

"That's very good of you," said Mum.

"I know," said Rosie. "I've got to start saving all over again, now. I s'ppose you actually *need* my money what I gave you?"

"Oh, now, Rosie," said Mum, "don't ruin it!"

She *is* a spoilt brat; but I was so happy at that moment that I was willing to forgive her.

At six o'clock Cupcake's mum arrived, with Joey. Mum said, "Come in, love! Come and sit down, have a cup of tea. You look worn out." It was true. I don't usually notice much about grown-ups, but even I could see that Cupcake's mum had obviously had a really tiring day. Dad said, "I'll put the kettle on," and went through to the kitchen, while Cupcake's mum sank on to the sofa and Mum lifted Joey out of his wheelchair and sat him down next to her. Cookie was all over him, giving little excited squeaks and covering him with loving doggy kisses. Joey tried ever so hard to respond, but the effort was too much for him. It's a long journey, up to London; and then, Cupcake told me, you had to travel for ages on the Underground to get to the hospital. I went on the Underground once. I thought it was quite fun, but I expect it might not be if you had to cope with a wheelchair.

"I don't know how you managed," said Mum.

Cupcake's mum said it was a case of having to. "But

people were very kind. There was always someone to help me with the stairs."

"Even so... I'm not surprised you're all washed up! You'd think the least they could do would be to provide you with transport."

Cupcake's mum smiled, a bit wearily, and said, "They probably expect you to take taxis."

"They think everyone's made of money." Mum sounded quite fierce about it. "Anyway," she perched on the arm of the sofa, "how did it go?"

"Oh..." Cupcake's mum waved a hand, like *I don't want to talk about it.*

"Well, the girls have one piece of good news," said Mum, "don't you?" She turned to me and Cupcake. "Lisa, go on! Tell your mum."

"We've got the money," said Cupcake. "Cookie can have his operation!"

"Really?" Cupcake's mum sat up. "You actually managed to raise it all?"

"Every penny," I said.

"I can't believe it!"

"I've got it right here," said Cupcake, "in my – " she glanced round, to make sure Dad hadn't come back – "in my knickers!"

She hadn't been able to think of anywhere else safe enough, so she'd put the notes in an envelope and Sellotaped it right round herself.

"Good heavens," said Mum. "How uncomfortable is that?"

Cupcake giggled and said, "Very!"

"But it's a lot of money," I said. "We couldn't risk losing it."

"Well, no," agreed Mum. "Not after all the trouble you've been to to get it."

"They were going to sit for a whole hour without moving," said Cupcake's mum. "Can you imagine? This pair? Not moving?"

"People kept prodding us," I said, "and trying to make us jump."

"But we didn't," said Cupcake.

"No, we just *sat*."

It wasn't really telling lies; we did just sit. Well, for fifteen minutes.

After much furtive fiddling, and keeping one eye on the door, Cupcake succeeded in unsticking herself from the envelope and held it out to her mum.

"All in notes!" said her mum. "How did you manage that?"

Cupcake didn't hesitate. She didn't even blush. "We took it to the Office and Mrs Mlada changed it for us."

I was impressed! Cupcake is usually such a *truthful* sort of person. Of course it is good to be truthful; I try to be truthful myself, most of the time. But just occasionally, like in an emergency, I think you have to be prepared to tell a few white lies. Cos that's all they were: white lies. It wasn't like we'd done anything wrong. And it made Cupcake's mum so happy! She put her arm round Joey and said, "Did you hear that? The girls have got the money for Cookie's operation. He's going to be all right!"

Joey was so tired he could hardly move, but he managed to give Cookie a little pat and tell him the good news: "Cookie's going be all right!"

Cupcake's mum asked us to say a big thank you to everyone who had contributed. "Tell them how grateful we are."

Rosie couldn't keep quiet any longer. She'd been remarkably restrained until then, but now it all burst out. She bounded forward, going, "I gave money! I gave *all my savings.*"

Mum said, "Rosie, we don't boast about our good deeds! We do them, and we keep quiet."

"Why?" Rosie turned on Mum indignantly. "I want people to know!"

Cupcake's mum said she was quite right, people ought to know. "And as soon as Cookie's over his operation we'll have a special celebratory tea and say a real proper thank you!"

Rosie smirked. She sent this triumphant glance in Mum's direction. She is such a brat! But I didn't really mind. Cupcake's mum said she would ring the vet first thing in the morning and fix a date for the operation.

"I'll see if they can fit him in on Wednesday. The sooner the better."

That night was the first night in ages that I went to bed without my head humming and buzzing with mad activity, all my brain cells working overtime to solve problems. There weren't any problems any more. We'd solved them all! Or so we thought...

CHAPTER NINE

Next morning, we stuck a big notice on our class notice board:

> WE HAVE RAISED ENOUGH MONEY FOR COOKIE TO HAVE HIS OPPIRATION. THANK YOU TO EVERYBODY FROM DANI AND LISA.

I had printed it off on the computer last night and was secretly quite proud of it. There was absolutely *no* call for Mr Wendell, who is our history teacher, to point out that the word "operation" was spelt wrongly. I mean, what did it matter? Teachers are always doing this; they just can't seem to stop *teaching*. I suppose it is what they are there for, but really it's like they're obsessed.

"Apart from that," said Mr Wendell, "who is Cookie and why does he need an operation?"

Eagerly, Cupcake explained. "He's our dog, he's a Beagle, and he has this bad leg. He's got this thing called..." Her voice trailed off. Her mum had told us what it was called, but Cupcake had obviously forgotten, and so had I. "It's like somewhere in Australia. What's in Australia?"

Emily, who was standing nearby, said, "Melbourne? Sydney? Perth?"

"Perth!" Cupcake snatched at it gratefully. "He's got this thing called Perthe's."

"Ah, I know it!" Mr Wendell nodded. "Perthe's disease. Named after one of the people who first discovered it. It's where there's an insufficient blood supply to the head of the femur."

You see what I mean? *Can't stop teaching.* But this time I forgave him, cos he went on to tell us that his Jack Russell had suffered from the same thing. "And now he's right as rain! Racing around like a lunatic, on all four legs."

It's funny, with teachers. What with them always being so busy teaching, and telling you what to do, and what not to do, and getting mad if you go and break some stupid rule, or forget just once in a while to do your homework, you don't tend to think of them as normal human beings who love their dogs, and their kids, and their mums and dads. Whenever I look at Mr Wendell now, I see him with his Jack Russell, racing around like a lunatic. Cupcake said to me, later, that she was glad he'd told us about his dog. She said she'd been secretly worried that Cookie wouldn't ever be able to use his leg again, not even after the operation.

"It's made me feel loads happier!"

At the end of school we raced back to Cupcake's place to take Cookie for his walk. His last one before the operation! Cupcake's mum said, "Give him a good one… he's booked in at the vet's first thing tomorrow morning. That means no food after seven o'clock. We must all remember."

"Oh, poor Cookie!" I said.

But Cupcake said no, he was lucky. "He's going to be all right! He is, isn't he, Mum?"

"Absolutely," said her mum. "Though he's bound to be a bit sorry for himself immediately after the operation."

Cupcake said that was OK, because the worst would then be over. "And Joey will look after him!"

To get to the park you have to go down some steps and along a narrow passage between the houses. It's quite safe; there're almost always other people around. *Almost* always. Today there wasn't anyone; just me and

Cupcake. Which was when Shane Mackie jumped us…

He'd obviously been lying in wait. He stood there at the entrance to the passage, blocking our way. I said, "What d'you want?" Doing my best not to sound scared in spite of my insides all turning to mush.

Shane said, "I've got a bone to pick with you two!"

I said, "What?"

"I thought you told me that ring was clean?"

Indignantly I said, "It was! We polished it."

"You told me you hadn't *nicked* it."

"We didn't nick it! I already said… it came from Cupcake's gran. What's it to you, anyway?

"Enough of the lip!" Shane jabbed a finger in my face. I took a step backwards, treading on Cupcake as I did so. "This didn't come from no one's gran."

"It did so!" I said. "It's been in the family for centuries… it's an antique."

"Yeah? Well, it's a hot antique! It's stolen property. *On a list.* I can't deal with stuff like that, I'm on probation."

I felt like saying, "That's your problem," but I wasn't brave enough.

"Here!" He pulled the ring out of his pocket and thrust it at me like it was a hand grenade about to go off. "You wanna carry stolen property around with you, be my guest. I'm not gonna get caught with it on me. You can give me the money back and we'll just forget the whole thing."

I stammered, "We can't give you your money back, we've already spent it."

"Well, you'd better unspend it, double quick, or there'll be trouble!"

Behind me, Cupcake squeaked, "What s-sort of t-trouble?"

"Sort of trouble you don't want. Believe me! I'll give you till the end of the week. If you don't come up with the money by then—" He paused.

I said, "W-what?"

"I'd have no option but to go to the police and turn you in. Know what they do with first offenders? They put them in institutions. You wouldn't wanna go to an institution! Take my word for it. Little soft things like you, you wouldn't last five minutes. I'll give you till this time Friday. Be here. With the money. *Or else.*"

With that, he disappeared. Cupcake and me continued, in deathly silence, to the park. It was a long time before either of us spoke.

"What are we going to do?" whispered Cupcake. "We can't give the money back. Not now!"

"No, we can't," I said. "And we won't!" I said as fiercely as I could, to give myself courage. "We'll wait till Cookie's had his operation, then we'll... we'll make him an offer!"

Doubtfully, Cupcake said, "What sort of offer?"

"We'll tell him we'll pay by instalments." That's what Mum and Dad had done, when we had to have a new fridge and they couldn't afford one straight off. "Hire purchase," I said. Already I was starting to feel more confident. Everybody bought things on hire purchase! "50p a week; we'll pay him back in no time."

"Excuse me," said Cupcake, "but I don't think you know what you're talking about."

"Hire purchase is what I'm talking about!"

"50p a week is what you're talking about."

"That's all right, we can manage 50p! Just means going without stuff for a while. It's for *Cookie*," I said. "It's for *Joey*."

"Yes, and it'd take…" Cupcake paused, and I could see her doing silent sums in her head. "Three hundred weeks… that's over five years!"

I said, "That can't be right." I did some silent sums of my own. Well, on my fingers, actually. I only made it come to *thirty* weeks. Not even a whole year!

Cupcake looked at me pityingly. "You know what Mr Craigen says?"

Mr Craigen is our maths teacher. *He* says I'm a mathematical moron.

"Even if we paid a *pound* a week," said Cupcake, "it'd still take for ever. Even if—"

I said, "All right! You don't have to keep on."

"I'm not keeping on. I'm just *saying*."

"Well, don't! It's not helpful."

"So you say something!"

"I just did. I said we'd make an offer. *You* said—"

"I know what I said."

"In that case, just shut up about it!"

It's not like me and Cupcake to quarrel. Cookie became quite upset. He scrabbled at us, clutching at our legs, with his ears pulled back. We immediately felt guilty. Cupcake picked him up and we both crooned over him.

"Poor little *man*! Did we frighten you?"

I hate it when people talk soppily to babies. I think it is such an insult to their intelligence. The babies' intelligence, that is. But Cookie was only a little dog, and tomorrow he was going to have a *big* operation, and it didn't matter how much that horrible thug threatened us, we were not going to ask Cupcake's mum to cancel it. No way!

"We'll think of something," I said. "We'll get the money somehow!"

But how? I didn't have any ideas left! Even when I concentrated really hard and *squeezed* at my brain, nothing came out. All I did was get myself in a panic, great waves of it crashing and pounding inside my head. As soon as I got home I rushed to the safety of my room, barricading the door behind me in case Rosie suddenly came bursting in. I took the ring out of my pocket and stood there, my heart galloping, while I wondered what to do with it. I wasn't walking round with it in my shoe any more! Not now I knew it was officially classed as stolen property. In the end I had what *I* consider to be a stroke of genius, as they say. I took my old teddy bear, who was coming apart at the seams, and stuffed the ring deep inside him. Even Mum would have no reason to go prying into my old teddy, and she certainly wouldn't dare chuck him out. All the same, just knowing that it was there was pretty scary. Who was going to believe us if we said our dog had sicked it up? The old woman would only have to tell them she'd caught us trespassing in her garden and they'd immediately jump to the conclusion that we must have broken in and helped ourselves. No one would ever take our word over hers.

Dad's joke, calling us after his favourite movie, didn't seem so funny any more. The real Butch Cassidy and the Sundance Kid had been outlaws, wanted by the sheriff. Now we were, too. I spent all evening terrified in case there was a knock at the door, and when I met Cupcake for school next day she said that she had been exactly the same.

"I know they don't know who we are, but if they've gone and made a list, like Shane said, *it's on the list...* "

They'd have sent copies to all the jewellers' shops, asking them to keep a lookout.

"We didn't give our names," I said.

"No, but the man from the shop might remember what we looked like! They could do one of those things, where they get artists to draw you." She meant

Identikit. I'd seen it on television. "They could have posters of us!"

It was a frightening thought. We half expected to see big drawings of ourselves stuck in shop windows and plastered on bus shelters... **WANTED FOR ROBBERY**!

"It's not funny," moaned Cupcake.

I told her that I'd never said it was.

"You sniggered!"

I said, "That was nerves."

"So what are we going to do? We could be recognised at any moment!"

It wasn't even like we could disguise ourselves. Our mums would never let us dye our hair, and we were stuck with school uniform whether we liked it or not.

"If we were Muslim," I said, "we could wear a hijab and cover ourselves up."

"Well, we're not," said Cupcake.

"I said if we *were*. You don't have to bite my head off."

"I'm not biting your head off, but what's the point of saying if we *were* when we're *not?*"

She was right: there wasn't any point. But she still didn't have to snap! "What's your solution?" I said. "Go to Mexico?"

It's what they do in movies when the police are after them: they flee to Mexico. If they live in America, that is, which most people seem to. In movies, I mean. It's obviously easier to be an outlaw in America. Where could me and Cupcake flee to? Scotland? The Isle of Wight?

"Stop being *stupid*," said Cupcake. "We could be arrested!"

Later on that day we thought we were going to be. Davina came bustling into the classroom, bursting with self-importance, to announce that she had seen *policemen* going into Reception. "Two of them! One man and one woman. Who d'you think they've come for?"

Emily pointed out that they hadn't necessarily come

for anyone. "They might just be going to give a talk on road safety, or drugs, or something." But Davina said no, they looked like they'd come to arrest someone.

Claire said, "How can you tell?"

"They had this sort of grim look," said Davina. And then she giggled and said, "Maybe they've come for you!"

I knew she was only saying it because it was the sort of thing she *would* say; I knew it didn't mean anything. All the same, it made me feel like someone had released a load of butterflies in my stomach. I glanced at Cupcake, and wished I hadn't. Her face had gone all pinched and white and sort of... *tragic*. I very quickly looked away again, before someone could notice and ask us what was wrong.

We spent all the rest of the day in fear and trembling, waiting to be dragged out of school in handcuffs. Halfway through geography, the door opened and Mrs Mlada came in. I sat hunched at my desk, not daring to look in Cupcake's direction. I was sure that she had come for us. After speaking in this *very low mutter* to Mr Hadley she went out again, leaving me and Cupcake convinced we were both going to be arrested the minute we set foot outside the classroom.

At lunch time we were so scared that we hid in the toilets, hunched up together in one cubicle. We learnt afterwards that the police had come about a boy in Year 10 who was always getting into trouble; it was nothing whatsoever to do with me and Cupcake being on their Wanted list. It was a great relief, though, as Cupcake said, it was only a matter of time. We couldn't *keep* hiding in the toilets.

As soon as school let out we raced like the wind back to Cupcake's place, partly cos we didn't feel safe out on the streets where people might recognise us, but mostly cos we wanted to make sure Cookie was all right after his operation. We found him curled up on the sofa, next to a beaming Joey. His poor leg was all shaved and had a big row of stitches, but he managed to give us a little wag and a lick. Cupcake's mum said that he was still a bit sleepy from the anaesthetic. "But it's been done, and the vet said he's going to be fine. So good work, girls! It's all thanks to you, and I think Joey would like to give you both a *big kiss*."

In that moment I knew that it had all been worth it. What did it matter if me and Cupcake got arrested? Who cared if we didn't last five minutes in an institution? We'd made one sick little boy very happy, and nothing could change that! I said this to Cupcake as she came to the gate with me. She agreed. She said that seeing Joey and Cookie together had convinced her that what we had done was right, even if it did mean we were criminals. She said, "I don't care what they do to us!"

"Me neither," I said; and I went off home feeling really brave. Unfortunately, it all crumbled the minute I got through the door, when Mum announced that we were going to go into town on Thursday after school and get me a new pair of shoes. "You can't go on wearing trainers any more. You know you're not supposed to."

I thought, *Go into town? I can't go into town!* "Mum, it's all right," I said, "it doesn't matter. Honestly! Nobody notices. Loads of people wear trainers. People wear trainers all the time. More people wear trainers than almost anything else. Mum, you can't *afford* to get me new shoes!"

Mum seemed to think this was quite funny. She said, "Since when have you not wanted to go out and have money spent on you?"

Piously I said, "It's Rosie's birthday next month. I'd sooner you spent it on her."

"That's a very sweet thought," said Mum, "but I think we can just about manage a birthday present for Rosie as well as a new pair of shoes for you. We're not that broke."

I felt like saying in that case I'd rather have the cash; at least it would go *some* way to paying Shane his money back. In desperation, I suggested that Mum could go by herself. "You don't need me there! You know what size I take."

"We are not buying shoes," said Mum, "without you trying them on. What's the matter, all of a sudden? You usually love going shopping!"

"I'm bored," I said. "Why can't we go somewhere else, for a change?"

"Like jumping in the car and driving all the way into London?"

"Mum, *could* we?" I said. But of course she'd only been joking. She was determined to drag me into the shopping centre. It was the last place I wanted to go! If the man from the jeweller's shop saw me, he'd have me arrested on the spot. Somehow, I wasn't feeling quite so brave any more.

There was only one thing for it, we had to get rid of the evidence. Not just get rid of it. *Hand it in.* Go to the nearest police station, and say—

What? What could we say? *Here is this ring that we thought you ought to have?* They'd want to know where it had come from and why we'd tried to sell it, cos by now the man in the jeweller's shop would have told them about us. "Said it belonged to one of their grandmothers."

Even if we told them the truth, and even if they believed us, they'd still want to know why we'd told lies about it. "So why did you say it belonged to your grandmother? You knew all along, didn't you, that it wasn't yours to sell? You knew you should have come to us!"

I suppose we *had* known; sort of. Anyway, going to the police wouldn't solve the problem of Shane and his money. He wouldn't rest until he'd had his revenge.

We had to get him his money back! Somehow, we just had to, it was the only way to be safe. And there was only one way I could think of doing it...

CHAPTER TEN

I told Cupcake my plan as we walked into school together next morning. "We'll get the ring, and we'll take it back to Lady Neverpoop, and—"

Cupcake said, "*Who?*"

"Lady Neverpoop!" It does make me so mad when she interrupts. "The old woman!"

"She's a *lady*?"

"Well—" Suddenly doubtful, I said, "It's what Mum calls her."

"Lady Neverpoop!" Cupcake giggled. "It's funny!"

Now it was my turn to lecture *her* about giggling. I said, "There's nothing funny about it. We've got to get Shane his money back, and we've got to get rid of the ring. If we don't get Shane his money he could do something really mean. He could do something to Cookie! And if we don't get rid of the ring and the police come and search the flat, they'll be bound to find it — they always find everything. They know all the places where people put things, like under the mattress, and in vases, and under the floorboards. They'd turn the place upside down; you can't hide anything from them! So what I'm saying—"

"We've got to give her ring back."

"Yes! We'll tell her truth... Cookie sicked it up. We'll say we're sorry we didn't bring it sooner but we didn't know that it was hers. It was only when we stopped and thought about it that we realised."

"Mm." Cupcake nodded, though not very enthusiastically.

"That way, we can't be accused of stealing."

"But what about the money? We still won't have the money!"

"We'll ask *her* for it. We'll tell her she owes it to us. For all we know, there might even be a reward!"

"You reckon?"

"I dunno. There might be. People usually give rewards."

"Mm." Cupcake nodded again, even less enthusiastic than before.

"We've got to do *something*," I said. "And unless you can think of anything better—" Which of course she couldn't.

Glumly she said, "So when d'you want to do it?"

I told her, as soon as possible. "I can't stand all the tension!"

Cupcake said she was surprised that criminals didn't all have nervous breakdowns, waiting for the police to come battering at their door and drag them away in handcuffs. I said that after a while they probably got used to it. "Everyone has to start somewhere."

"I never wanted to start at all!"

I said, "Neither did I, and it's worse for me – I'm the one with the incriminating evidence."

There was a pause, then Cupcake said: "You mean, the ring?"

"Yes, I've hidden it in my—"

"Don't tell me, don't tell me!" She stuffed her fingers in her ears. "I don't want to know!" And then she looked ashamed and said, "In case they question me... I might break under pressure."

We both would. I might last out a *little* while longer, as I am not quite so easily intimidated, but I knew they would break even me in the end. They always break everybody. They shine bright lights in your face and won't let you sleep. Urgently I said, "We'll do it immediately after school. We'll go back to my place and get it – *the thing* – and take it straight round to her."

Cupcake sighed. "All right. If you think that's best."

I knew she wasn't happy about it so I wasn't surprised, when the time came, that she started to waver. "Maybe we ought to take Cookie out first? Maybe we should wait till after tea? Maybe it doesn't need to be both of us? Cos I was a bit rude to her, you know? It'd probably be better if it was just you."

"I'm not doing it by myself," I said.

"Maybe we shouldn't do it at all!"

I fixed her with this cold, hard stare. "You'd rather run the risk of Cookie being hurt?"

That got to her. She said she was sorry for being such a wimp, and *of course* she would come with me. We went into my bedroom and Cupcake screwed her eyes tight shut while I fished the ring out of my old teddy and stuffed it back in my shoe for safekeeping. Just in case; I mean, you never know. People get mugged all the time. It would be a total disaster if we lost the ring.

We told Mum we were going to collect Cookie and

take him for a walk. Mum seemed surprised. She said, "Is he ready for walks?" I assured Mum that we would only go just a little way — gentle exercise, the vet had said — and whispered to Cupcake that we would pick him up afterwards."

On our way round the block, we bumped into Shane. I'm sure he'd been waiting for us. He didn't say anything; just looked at us. Me and Cupcake did our best to ignore him, but the minute we were round the corner we ran.

I'd been rehearsing all day what I was going to say to the old woman — whose name, I now realised, was *not* Lady Neverpoop. I felt really stupid for ever thinking it was. But I'd worked out what to say, and I said it! All in a rush. "Excuse us for not bringing this back before but our dog that you gave us cos of not wanting to be bothered with him any more, well, he sicked it up and we didn't realise that it was yours, but now that we do we've come to give it back and we wondered, please, if there was a reward?"

Well! You'd have thought she'd be so pleased to have the thing back, and so impressed with our honesty, that she would have been only too eager to give us a reward. Instead, quite crossly, she said, "You expect a *reward* for doing your civic duty? People who *expect* do not *deserve*. Had you not been quite so brazen I might perhaps have considered the possibility. As it is, most certainly not!"

Just for a moment I didn't know what to say. That was when Cupcake jumped in. "Most people give rewards," she said. It wasn't the most *helpful* of remarks, but I felt grateful to her for trying.

"We didn't have to bring it back," I said.

"If you hadn't brought it back it would be stealing, and you could get into a great deal of trouble."

"Like my mum's friend who used to clean for you," I said. "She was ever so upset when you accused her of stealing."

"Yes – well! That was unfortunate. If you had come to me sooner—"

"We couldn't," I said. "It was still inside our dog."

"Our dog that you gave us," prompted Cupcake.

The old woman raised an eyebrow. Just one. I wish I could do that! "What exactly," she demanded in this really icy voice, "are you trying to say? Are you daring to suggest that in some way my ring belongs to you? I hardly think that would hold up in a court of law!"

"What we're trying to say…" It came bursting out of Cupcake in a great torrent. "My mum had to pay the vet almost £300 for an operation and she didn't have £300 so we had to borrow some of it from someone cos Cookie was really *sick*, and now the person that we borrowed it from is threatening us!"

By now the tears were streaming down Cup's face. I would have been too proud to cry, but Cup is someone who cries quite easily. Just as well, as it happens! For the first time *ever*, the old woman stopped looking grim and disagreeable. "Now, why didn't you tell me this right at the start?" she said. "It would have been so much better than simply trying to blackmail me into giving you a reward. How much did your mother have to borrow?"

"It wasn't her mum," I said, "it was us. We borrowed £225 from this boy who lives on the Estate and he's given us till Friday to pay it back. He's a really horrible sort of person! He'd mug you soon as look at you."

The old woman frowned. "Have you told your parents?"

"No!" I shook my head wildly. "They think we got the money from people at school. We did this thing where we didn't speak for a whole day and people sponsored us."

"But it wasn't enough," sobbed Cupcake, "and Cookie had to have his operation otherwise Mum said we'd have to find him another home with someone who could afford it, and my little brother's got muscular dystrophy and he loves Cookie *so much*—"

"Enough!" The old woman raised her hand. "I have heard enough. You're starting to make my head ache.

You had better tell this person, whoever he is, that if he wants his money he can call round here, with you — both of you! — at four o'clock on Friday. Not a minute earlier, not a minute later. Four o'clock *on the dot*. Can you be trusted to arrange that?"

I gulped and nodded. Cupcake abruptly stopped crying and stood, open-mouthed. And then we both remembered our manners and went, "*Thank you!*"

"Honesty brings its own rewards," said the old woman. "Not everyone would have returned my property. I'm very glad that you did. It's an heirloom, you know. It means a lot to me."

"It's very pretty," said Cupcake shyly.

The old woman smiled. "It is," she said, "isn't it? It used to belong to my mother." And then she got all grim again and said, "Very well, then. Friday at four o'clock. Please be sure that you get here on time. And thank you again for being so honest."

"We weren't really," whispered Cupcake, as we made our way home.

"We were *in the end,*" I said. "That's all that matters."

Shane was still hanging around, leaning against a wall at the entrance to the Estate. He mouthed one word: *Friday.*

"You can stop threatening us," I said. "We've arranged for you to get your money back."

He looked at me, eyes narrowed. "What's that supposed to mean?"

"Just meet us here at 4 o'clock, Friday," I said. "And make sure you're on time."

Shane said, "Why? Where you gettin' the cash from?"

"What's it to you?" said Cupcake. And then she immediately turned bright scarlet and went scurrying off in a panic, alarmed by her own daring.

Shane ignored her. He didn't deal with Cupcake, he dealt with me. I was the one that talked the talk.

"Just be here," I said. "OK?"

His eyes had gone almost to slits. "How do I know

it's not a set-up?" Talk about suspicious! But I suppose, if you're a criminal, you have to be. You just never know when someone's going to rat you out. "Come on!" he said. "How are you getting your hands on £225?"

I told him it was being given to us by someone we knew. "We've got to go and pick it up from her, and you've got to come with us. And you'd just better watch your manners," I said, "cos she's a *lady*."

Shane sneered, curling his top lip into a hoop. "Think I'm bothered?"

I said, "You'd better be!" and went scooting off after Cupcake. Just knowing that Lady Neverpoop was going to repay him his rotten money was such a *huge weight* off my mind it made me feel quite bold. Shane Mackie didn't frighten me! And I bet he wouldn't frighten old Lady Neverpoop, either, even if she wasn't an actual real lady.

I was right: he didn't! He stood there on her doorstep looking all sullen and aggressive, and she just kind of *froze* him. She said, "Here is your money, young man. Take it, and be gone! And we'll have no more threats, if you please."

Cupcake said afterwards that she almost felt sorry for him. "Cos, I mean, it *was* his money. It did belong to him."

"You've got to be joking!" I said.

Cupcake thought about it and said yes, perhaps she was. "Probably didn't come by it honestly."

"Most likely mugged someone."

"Maybe he'll get put in prison?" said Cupcake.

I said that we could always hope.

That was ages ago, and we're still hoping! Well, I am; Cupcake is too soft. She changed her mind when we discovered, just the other day, that he is working in the local supermarket. I'd gone in to get something for Mum. I couldn't believe it when I saw Shane there, stacking shelves. He caught my eye and then looked away. I think secretly he was a bit ashamed, being caught doing an ordinary job the same as anyone else. When I told Cupcake she said maybe he wasn't a criminal any more. I went "Huh!" but Cupcake said you have to give people the benefit of the doubt. "I hope you didn't say anything mean to him?"

I said, "*Me?*"

"Like laughing at him, or something. Not if he's trying to sort himself out."

I sometimes think that Cupcake is far too *nice*. But it's good that one of us is. She is the softie, I am the hard nut! I guess that is why we work so well together. Every time we look at Cookie, we congratulate ourselves. He is racing around on all four legs now, just as Mr Wendell promised he would. Joey is so proud of him, he introduces him to everyone he meets as "My dog, Cookie, who's had a big operation." They're still the best of friends, just like me and Cupcake. They can't bear to be separated. The very first thing Cookie does when we bring him back from a walk is jump on to Joey's lap and lick him all over, barking and wagging his tail like they haven't seen each other for weeks. But he is always very gentle. With me and Cupcake he behaves like a normal rough and tumble puppy who tugs and wrestles and even, occasionally, gives us a nip when he gets a bit over-excited. He's never, ever like that with Joey. He seems to know that Joey is different, and special.

Everyone knows that Joey is special. Even Rosie, who told me just the other day that she'd been thinking about it and she was *glad* she'd given us all her savings so that Joey and Cookie could be together. She said, "When I see them I don't mind so much about having to start all over again. I still wish I didn't have to, but I don't *really* mind. Cos it's for Joey."

Even old Lady Neverpoop (I always call her that, even though I know it's not her real name). Even though she's crabby as ever. Mum's mate Trudi went back to work for her, for *loads more money*, and says she still treats her like dirt. But we walked past her house a while ago, with Cookie on the lead, and Joey in his wheelchair, and she was in her front garden. Cupcake wanted to cross the road to get away from her, but Joey caught sight of her and immediately waved and cried, "My dog, Cookie!" and she actually stopped what she was doing, and came to the gate, and patted Cookie on the head, and *smiled.* She said she was glad to see that he had recovered from his operation, and then guess what? She gave Joey £5 to get Cookie some treats! So she obviously isn't all bad.

As for me and Cupcake, we have decided that we are definitely not cut out to be criminals. We both think that once is enough! From now on, we are determined to go straight.

We have also made a vow to try and stop calling each other Fudge and Cupcake, but it is proving quite difficult. I blame Dad! When I suggested that perhaps I shouldn't be Fudge Cassidy any more he just laughed and said, "All right, you sensitive little flower. How about Button?"

Button, I ask you!!! How can you hope to be a celeb

with a dad that calls you *Button*? When I told Cupcake she said did that mean she'd have to be called Door Knocker. "Then we could be Button and Door, like some sort of comedy act."

I don't think so! We'll probably just stick to Fudge and Cupcake. It seems easier, somehow. In any case, we've kind of got used to it.

STAR CRAZY ME!

I've wanted to be a pop star ever since I can
remember - well, a rock star, actually, as I have a really
BIG voice. My nan used to say, *"That girl is star crazy!"*

I was sooo excited when I heard about the school talent
contest. I even wrote a special song with my friend Josh.
But then the meanest girl in the universe called me
a fat freak. I stormed out of school, and now I just
don't want to go back...

978 0 00 715619 7

The Secret Life of
SALLY TOMATO

A is for armpit,
Which smells when you're hot,
Specially great hairy ones,
They smell A LOT.

Hi! Salvatore d'Amato here – call me Sal if you must –
and I am not writing a diary! I'm writing the best
alphabet ever. An alphabet of Dire and Disgusting Ditties.

I'm up to two letters a week, and I reckon it will take me
the rest of term to complete my masterpiece. By then I
plan to have achieved my Number One aim in life – to
find a girlfriend. After all, I'm already twelve, so I can't
afford to wait much longer…

978 0 00 675150 4

www.harpercollins.co.uk

www.jeanure.com

PASSION FLOWER

**Of course, Mum shouldn't have
thrown the frying pan at Dad.
The day after she threw it,
Dad left home...**

Stand back! Family Disaster Area! After the Frying Pan
Incident, it looks like me and the Afterthought are going
to be part of a single-parent family. Personally, I'm on Mum's side
but the Afterthought is Dad's number one fan. Typical.
Still, Dad's got us for the whole summer and things are
looking promising: no rules, no hassle, no worries.
But things never turn out the way you think.

978 0 00 715619 7

www.harpercollins.co.uk

Printed by RR Donnelley at Glasgow, UK